Tide Song

Tide Song:
Melody of the Deep

Book One of the Tide Song Duology

K. E. Hummel

Copyright © 2024 K. E. Hummel
All rights reserved.
ISBN: 979-8-9916813-2-2
Developmental Editor: Joanie Lorraine Haines
Book Cover Artist: Bia Andrade

For information address Heart Tide Press at **info@tidepress.net**

www.tidepress.net

First *Heart Tide Press* paperback printing: January 2025
Second Edition, *Heart Tide Press*: March 2025

To my family and friends, for always believing in me. And to Joanie Lorraine, who pulled me from the raging sea.

Contents

The Nadako Sea

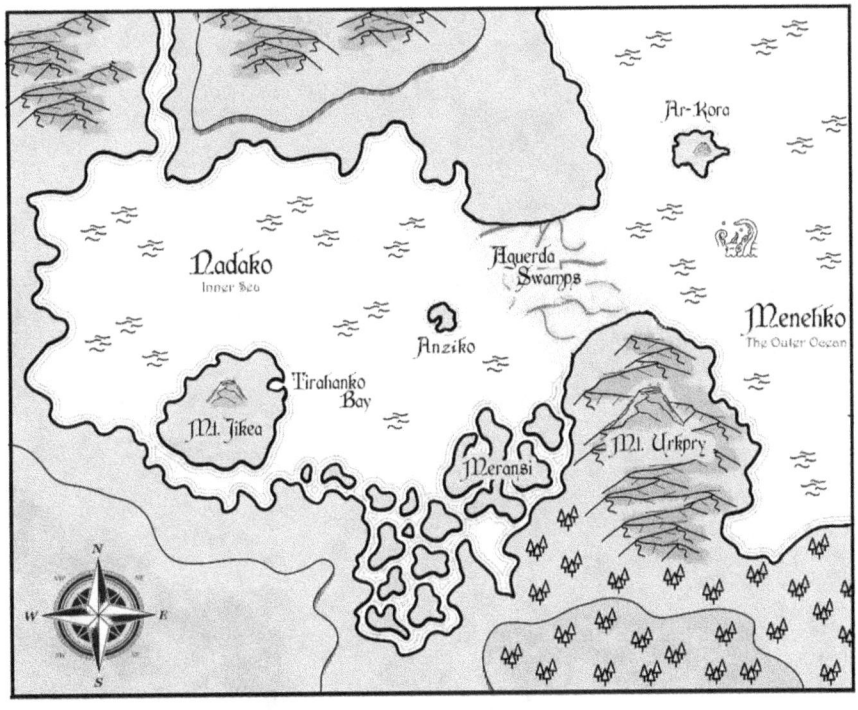

Prologue: Something Comes

*S*wimsAbove curled her tentacles around her eggs, skin crinkling into rose-colored bumps that mimicked the coral rocks sheltering her nest. The ocean current's ebb and flow no longer held meaning for *SwimsAbove*. She was deep into brooding season, huddled on her nest, protecting her unborn younglings. Not eating. Not moving. Slowly dying so that her children might live. Such was the way of a wild octopus, solitary and alone in the vastness of the outer ocean.

But *SwimsAbove* was a *kopri*, a being of intellect and language, not just some mindless octopus. Her mate perched on the top of a white coral spire; eyes alert and swiveling for danger. He was her Guardian, and she knew that as long as he lived, he would protect her and their nest with his life — despite instincts urging him to leave.

Like *SwimsAbove*, her Guardian was also a kopri, and his fierce mind ruled his body. Throughout this long brooding season, he had suppressed the instinct to leave, refusing to abandon his mate and their eggs. Unlike a primitive octopus, her mate returned to their nest time after time, bringing food and driving off predators, protecting the nest until their younglings could hatch, allowing *SwimsAbove* and her mate to return to the gentle waters of the inner sea.

She kept one eye open, swiveled upward toward her Guardian. Unbidden, a yellow flash smiled across her skin, responding to the rings of black pulsing beneath her mate's eyestalks. She read her name there, painted on the skin of his mantle, that bullet-shaped sac trailing from his head. The mantle could contract, creating a blast of water jetting him through the sea. Or expand, creating a sack to engulf his prey and draw it to his razor-sharp beak.

"*SwimsAbove,*" her mate signed, texture and color rippling over his body as he disappeared into the coral. "*Grow still! Something comes.*"

She remained silent, her mantle motionless as it took on the color and shape of the seabed floor. The currents shifted. Tiny fish came first, swimming unaware past the ocean's deadliest hunter. A swarm of thousands glittering like diamond specks scattered through the sea.

Her mate turned one eyestalk. Slowly. Patiently. And when dozens of fat prey fish approached his hiding spot, devouring the tiny specks, he leapt—tentacles thrusting—launching into the center of the unsuspecting school of prey. His mantle flared wide, engulfing two fish, which struggled in his grip. His beak struck once, twice, then triumph flashed in turquoise rings down his tentacles, which gripped two meaty fish.

The school of prey escaped, silver bellies flashing in sunlight streaming from the ocean's surface, the deadly hunter already forgotten. They were prey—just fish—without a Kopri's keen mind.

"*SwimsAbove!*" her mate signed, jetting toward her hiding place, the swirls and knobs of her name written on his body.

Her eyes flew open, pink highlights rippling over her skin as her mate returned. She longed to swim to him and entwine her tentacles with his, but she could not leave the nest—even for a moment.

And so, she waited, flashing his name over and over on the mantle beneath her eyes.

* * *

With a final surging pulse, the Guardian finished his hunt and returned to their nest. He wrapped his tentacles around *SwimsAbove*, embracing her and pushing the captured prey toward her beak.

The Guardian kept still while she ate, feeling the firmness of her body coiled within his, blocking his view of their eggs. He sensed their hatching time was near. Soon his younglings would swim away, their minds slowly developing in the unique water of the spawning grounds. After that, he and

SwimsAbove could return to the inner sea, which their human friends called *Nadako*.

This was a moment the Guardian would cherish during the long and lonely years of his life, this final moment of peace and beauty with his nest and mate held safely in his grasp. And the kopri spawning grounds, glittering in sunlight streaming from the surface of the ocean.

But in all the years that followed, the image seared into his mind was of the shadow looming over his nest.

A darkness blocking the light.

Something moving on the surface, up in the world of wind and air and humans — but not his human friends and allies from the Nadako Sea.

These strange humans from the outer ocean had no names and could sing no Nadako words. They could read no colored patterns painted on a kopri mantle. They were mute, unthinking beasts.

He turned toward the edge of darkness, where the deep water swallowed the world. A cloud burst from the seabed. Frantic fish swam toward him. Shrimp and lobster and crab scrambling away from approaching doom.

The Guardian's tentacles slowly uncurled, lingering a moment before releasing his mate from his protective grasp.

"*Something comes,*" he signed to her. "*Stay hidden.*"

Camouflage rippled on her flesh as he surged toward danger. He swiveled one eyestalk backward, seeking

SwimsAbove, but she had already pressed herself flat against their nest, vanishing from sight.

Satisfied that his mate was hidden, the Guardian jetted forward, ignoring the maddened prey fleeing past him. He swam toward devastation blooming from chains that hung from the surface, dragging across the seabed.

His eyes darted everywhere, until the scouring weight of metal links burned into his vision—a heavy descending line grinding into the white feathery branches of a coral spire, smashing the delicate structure which crumbled and fell to the ocean floor. The snaking cable continued, ripping through corals that had grown inch by inch over centuries.

He turned an eye toward the surface where dozens of ruinous chains descended from the shadow covering his world.

The cold metal links passed by, revealing a vast net scraping toward him, its weighted end grinding over the seafloor. The oncoming net engulfed terrified fish, scuttling crabs, and predators too dim-witted to escape.

A cloud of white silt engulfed him, and he felt currents sucking him toward the net. For a moment, instinct gripped him, and he almost fled. But then a chain swung past, pushing water against his tentacles. The murderous links moved on, breaking coral and crushing crabs beneath their weight. Heading directly toward his nest and his unprotected eggs and mate!

The Guardian snapped his mantle shut, creating a blast of water that sent him rocketing past the chain. When he arrived above the nest, he fought down an animal instinct to flee. He turned and faced the oncoming chain, which drove forward without mercy — sparing nothing.

He held himself still. Both eyes turned, focusing on the approaching destruction. Then he launched forward, all his energy and effort driving him toward the uncaring metal links. Three of his tentacles wrapped around its cold iron rings, while the others whirled, pushing against the water. His mantle expanded and contracted, a powerful jet slowly moving the chain away from his mate and eggs.

He strained against the rough links, which tore into his flesh, leaving a long bloody gash beneath his eyes. The chain moved sideways, dragging across the seabed floor inches from his nest.

Relief swept over him — until he looked up.

Until he peered through a cloud of his own blood at a massive net filling his vision. Frantic fish were caught in its mesh, fins trapped, gills gasping. The net spared no living creature, not even a helpless shark, flailing wildly in the deadly web.

The Guardian ignored the pain throbbing from his wound and turned his eyes forward, staring at the weighted net grinding over the world.

At that moment, his mind turned to ice. There was no escape for his nest. Nor was there any escape for the fish caught in the vast rope web, which rose, dragging its catch into the poisonous air.

"*SwimsAbove!*" he signed, his flesh turning black with fear. "*We must flee!*"

She signed nothing in reply, spreading herself flatter over their nest, mantle and tentacles stiffening, seeking to protect their eggs.

He pleaded with her, gripping her tentacles and pulling. But she had anchored herself to the reef, covering their eggs, and would not move.

He stayed, watching the net weights grind closer. Watching the net as it entangled barracuda and prey fish alike.

Clouds of debris filled the sea, blinding him. When the first knots of the tangled lattice brushed his probing, outstretched tentacle, instinct overwhelmed him. He fled, blasting away from their nest until his mind finally regained control of his body.

He stopped, turning back to face the strangling woven lines. And there he saw her, *SwimsAbove*, trapped in its lethal mesh. Her tentacles crushed and flailing, with his name flashing in red agony on her flesh.

He jetted upward and came level with her. But the net rose between them, dragging her into the world of air. He crested the surface, watching helplessly as her flesh turned black, pulsing red in agony. She disappeared over the edge of a massive floating human-made island as the invaders pulled in their prey.

SwimsAbove fell, vanishing from her Guardian's sight, never to be seen by anyone again.

His mantle deflated, and he sank into the deep.

The floating island and the net disappeared into the distance, while the Guardian scoured the seabed, seeking the nest he had guarded.

But in all the kopri spawning grounds, he only found broken shells, shattered dreams — and death.

* * *

In the lonely years ahead, he could never remember how long he lay exposed beside the shattered shells of his younglings, willing himself to die. Hours passed, then days. But finally, the grief subsided enough so that he could think again.

The black of fear slowly gave way on his flesh to the grey of despair.

Then, red streaks of anger formed, flashing like lightning along his tentacles.

And finally: his skin pulsed purple.

He was Kopri! Not some mindless fish.

And so, he rose from the destruction of his nest and began swimming after the floating island, leaving the devastated kopri spawning grounds behind him.

His grief settled into a deep anger as he swam away. The Guardian was alone and consumed by grief, but determination filled him. He would fight! He would find his mate's murderers and put an end to the destruction caused by their floating islands. And so began the Guardian's quest. His name was

DeepRunner, and season after season, year after year, he sought allies and answers in the world above the waves.

But now, after twenty years of seeking a way to stop them, he was no closer to winning justice for his mate. And the only thing that he had really learned in those twenty years of struggle was the name of his enemy — the *Koru-Kah!*

Child of the Open Sea

Kei woke to the sound of her father grumbling from his sleeping mat. She levered upright onto her canes, nose twitching at the acrid fumes of burnt oil clinging to dozens of hand-carved drums cluttering the tiny hut.

She glared at a stone pipe lying beside her father, then turned away, feet dragging beneath her slim body. She leaned on one cane at a time, swinging rigid legs from hips until she reached the open door of the hut—built within arm's reach of the Nadako sea.

Her father's voice called after her. "For once," he said gruffly, "just do what your mother wants. Would it hurt you to go to Tirahanko Bay tonight and sing in her choir?"

Kei stood in the hut's doorway with her eyes closed. For a moment, she wanted only to obey her father — to go and sing on the black sand beach of Tirahanko, where her kopri friends floated in the center of the bay — pushing their bulbous heads above the waves to catch each crystal note.

But then she remembered the eyes of her mother's choir, staring in pity at her stiff legs. Her jaw clenched, head shaking as she ignored her father and left his hut. The tips of her canes sank into hard packed sand as she struggled across a small cove — toward a kayak tied at the water's edge.

The kayak consisted of two thick reed bundles tapered at the front, forming a high, curved bow. There, a short-hafted fishing spear stood upright, lashed to the reeds. A woven seat created a backrest. She dropped onto the seat, pulling her resisting legs onto the center of the kayak. After strapping her canes to the hull, Kei took up her paddles, her powerful arms thrusting the sleek craft off the sand.

She drove the kayak into the surf, rigid legs forgotten, and paddled north up the wave-struck coast, past thick mangrove forests.

When the sun had moved a hand's width across the sky, she arrived at a narrow inlet leading into Tirahanko Bay. She passed between the inlet's basalt cliffs, entering the bay's protected waters. There, a platform carved long ago sat at the top of the cliffs, three times Kei's height above the water.

She tied her kayak to an outcropping, then began pulling herself up a knotted rope dangling from above. A grunt exploded from her lips with each strained movement. Her thighs struck the jagged rock as she climbed, one hand after another. Her arms burned as she hauled the useless weight of her legs up the cliffside. Finally, she reached the top, dragging herself over the smooth lip of a platform — carved long ago to help NetSingers, like her, track the hunt.

Lying face down against the stone, Kei released the rope and rolled over, staring up at the blue depths of an open sky.

A light wind dried sweat on her brow as she sat up. To her right, Tirahanko Bay stretched out before her, its black sand kissed by the restless surf, dense jungle pressing in from all sides. To her left, the open ocean unfurled in rippling waves of pastel aquamarine, stretching endlessly under the warm sun. Her pounding heart steadied, eyes sweeping toward open water. There, dozens of human hunters in their reed sea-kayaks had launched westward, following their aquatic allies — who searched for prey beneath the waves.

Kei settled onto the NetSinger's Platform, drawing a deep breath to steady herself. Just then, a sudden splash near her kayak yanked her attention to a large kopri rising above the water.

"Morning light!" Kei sang out, pitching her trained falsetto voice high enough for the newcomer to hear. Behind the kopri's head a muscular sack bulged. This sack — their mantle — contained their hearts and lungs and organs. A thousand tiny bumps formed a green sign of greeting on the mantle's fluid, crinkling skin. The kopri reached one sinuous tentacle — longer than Kei's kayak—above the water. The rainbow-flecked tentacle tip wavered near the edge of the platform, then slapped downward, spraying drops of salt water across the cliffside.

Kei's lips curled into a smile as she read a joking comment written in shifting patterns of scrunched flesh on the kopri's mantle, which then flashed all colors at once in hysterical laughter.

"Only a kopri!" Kei sang brightly, her voice filled with amusement, "Would think that's funny!"

The tentacle slapped water one more time before slipping beneath the waves. The true name of a kopri had no translation, only textured patterns of color displayed on their bulbous mantle sacks, unique to each. But this was Kei's best friend, who her father—during happier times—had jokingly named *OldFish*.

"Go on," Kei sang to her friend. "It's time to hunt. You don't have to stay with me."

OldFish flashed yellow below their eyes—smiling in vibrant colors. *"I will stay. With you,"* her friend signed, before contracting their water-filled mantle. With a powerful burst, a jet of water propelled OldFish across the inlet to where a second kopri waited. Together, the two wrapped their suckered tentacles around the net, preparing for the hunters' return. Soon, the hunters would drive their prey into the bay, and the waiting pair would drag the net across the inlet, turning the shallow waters of Tirahanko into a sealed trap.

Kei's eyes wandered over the bay, to a wide beach edged with palm trees, where racks of gutted fish would soon hang, drying in the sun. In the far distance, the volcanic cone of Mt. Jikea rose into the sky, but Kei's duties lay out to sea. She turned away from land, eyes scanning the waves. From time to time she sang a note, alerting her two companions to what she saw. And when the first kayak began driving toward Tirahanko Bay, her song signaled the two waiting kopri to tighten their tentacled grips on the net.

The kayaking hunters' voices echoed over the water, too low pitched for their aquatic allies to hear. Kopri could hear only the highest tones — the chirping warning of a fiddler crab's claw rasping on its carapace, or the treble notes of a human woman skilled in shaping high-pitched frequency into song.

Kei squinted her eyes against the sun as she tracked the motions of the hunters. Many of the dozens of kopri had mantles larger than Kei. Their bodies swelled with water and then squeezed, creating powerful jets that propelled them beneath the waves, eight tentacles undulating behind their bullet-shaped heads.

Kei heard faint voices as the Kayaking hunters called to one another. The kopri surged below, driving a school of spikeback snapper toward the inlet. Fish erupted from the waves, dozens of arm-length silvery bodies leaping into the air, seeking to escape their relentless pursuers. But dozens of kayaks blocked their path, turning the school toward Tirahanko, while submerged kopri jetted behind, mantles glowing violet with excitement.

Kei sang out, keeping her two companions informed about the progress of the hunt. Together, kopri and human hunters drove the school of fish toward the bay. As the hunt approached, Kei leaned forward, the notes of her song warning her two crewmates to prepare to close the net.

The hunters drove the huge school of fish into the narrow strait leading into Tirahanko Bay. With kayaks chasing above and kopri pushing below, the only escape for the snapper school was forward. A mass of meaty fish seethed into the bay. And then both prey and hunters were through the strait and Kei sang out, high tones directing the two net-tenders to close the trap. Timing mattered. Many of the fleeing fish would escape unless the net closed quickly.

This was Kei's main job: without a human *NetSinger* tracking the progress of the hunt—and alerting the kopri who tended the nets—the trap might fail.

No matter what Kei's father said, the task was important.

Gray knobbed tentacles gripped cordage, dragging the net across the inlet, sealing off the exit from Tirahanko Bay. OldFish's clever tentacles wrapped lines around stanchions carved into the rock below the NetSinger's platform, pulling the net tight.

The hunt ended, and a feeding frenzy began. The bay's water boiled. Snappers leapt and plunged, trying to escape. But the kopri used their clever tentacles to drag one hapless fish after another into their mantles: squeezing, killing, plunging their beaks into flesh and eating at leisure.

The human hunters beached their kayaks on the sand, then leapt to smaller nets placed around the bay, waiting for their underwater partners to finish feasting.

After the kopri ate their fill, they gathered at the bay's entrance, serene blue patterns signaling their readiness to Kei, who sang back excitedly, "Wait."

When the last kopri finished their meal and joined the hunting pod, Kei sang to her two companions, who untied the net, opening the trap so that the hunting pod could return to the open sea. When the last of the hunters departed, Kei's two net-tending companions passed through, then tied the nets again, trapping the remaining fish for their human friends.

Before departing, OldFish rose to the surface, flashing excitedly. *"Come with me tonight. Join the celebration!"*

Kei read the flashing patterns on her friend's mantle. But the cascading colors sparked a painful image in Kei's mind—of tentacles reaching toward her, years ago—but she pushed that painful memory away, watching silently as her kopri friend swam off.

Alone again at the NetSinger's Platform, Kei grabbed the rope and lowered herself to the water. Taking up her paddle, she moved into Tirahanko Bay, where the human hunters had begun pulling in their nets—dragging mounds of spikeback snapper onto the black sand beach.

* * *

Later that day in the deeper water beyond Tirahanko, OldFish burrowed into deep coral, fearful black tentacles squeezing into cracks in the reef. Above, where sunlight pierced the waves, krill and plankton sparkled like tiny motes of dust shimmering in air. A group of elders were gathered near OldFish's hiding spot, surrounding an unknown Kopri, an ancient stranger who had come to Tirahanko Bay. The stranger ignored the greeting signs flashed by the elders of OldFish's hunting pod and offered none of its own.

Only orders. Demanding and insistent.

"*Summon your humans,*" the threatening old kopri flashed, purple lacing each sign. "*Call their **Singer** to me. I have a message all must hear.*"

A dozen Kopri pulsed slowly in the current, maintaining their positions, mantles gray and silent, until their leader sent rippling textures over their skin, flashing words to the stranger.

"*The humans are not ours to summon,*" the pod leader calmly signed, "*but we can ask our friends to join us in the bay.*"

"*Summon. Ask. Call it what you will,*" the old kopri replied, anger swirling in their words. But the pod leader remained steady, patiently replying, "*Why? You are free to speak to the humans yourself.*"

A ripple of annoyance swept over the stranger's body, which suddenly loomed large, tentacles slicing the water before spearing toward the pod leader.

In the hidden crevice, OldFish tensed, tentacles bunching, preparing to launch themselves out of the coral. The stranger was attacking the pod! Frightening as the ancient stranger was, the hunting pod swam together. What threatened one, threatened all.

Before OldFish could launch from the coral, the ancient stranger froze in the water, their skin turning the deepest grey of despair.

No one moved in the currents. The pod waited, tense and prepared to defend itself.

But the stranger shrank away, grey giving way to the sadness of blue painted on their skin. Black rings formed around the stranger's eyes: exhaustion too deep to hide.

OldFish relaxed, fear of the stranger giving way to compassion for the old Kopri's sadness: compassion for the scars on their skin, and the deep gash below one of their eyes, painting a history of suffering and pain clear for anyone to read.

Streaks of blue and black rippled down the stranger's tentacles, resignation coloring their bitter words: *"Tell them I have come from the Deep, with a prophecy of doom. I am DeepRunner, who has seen the end of days. And I need their help, or our people will disappear forever."*

Prophet of the Deep

That evening, Kei sat alone beneath the basalt cliffs surrounding Tirahanko Bay, near one of the warm pools smoothed by the constant tide. Laughter from the villagers echoed through the air as they relaxed in the natural hot springs. Meanwhile, dozens of Kopri floating in the center of the bay flashed joyful greens and yellows, basking in the heated water bubbling from cracks in the rocks.

Kei's fingers clenched the sand, her hand tightening and relaxing with each passing moment. She watched her father walk to his *summoning drum*—a hollowed log, half-submerged at the edge of the bay—its vibrations would call their aquatic allies to the celebration. She wished she could join him, but the thought of so many sympathetic eyes on her—watching her stiff legs struggle over the sand—kept her rooted in place. Men and boys held smaller hand drums and strike-stones, ready to follow the rhythm of the women's chorus — which stood nearby, voices tuned and ready.

Torches lit the scene, flames flickering as the sun dropped below Mt. Jikea, the cratered peak rising to the west of the bay. Once in every lifetime, that fierce mountain shook the earth, sending smoke and glowing lava down its jungle-covered slopes. But tonight, its fires were dark and silent.

As Kei faced the choir, a slim figure separated from the group, gliding toward her across the beach. Soon her mother, Ahmisha, reached her side, sitting gracefully beside her daughter. Kei held herself erect, painfully aware of her mother's effortless beauty. Together, they listened to the harmony of wind and waves, staring at the distant slopes of Mt. Jikea. Ahmisha moved closer, draping her arm around Kei, who leaned backward, refusing her mother's embrace. Ahmisha dropped her arm, breath escaping from between pursed lips.

"I'm glad you came," Ahmisha said, a hint of rejection filling her words.

"It's my right!" Kei replied abruptly. "I hunted!"

For a moment, Ahmisha did not reply, choosing her words carefully before saying, "I know you did. And you can join the hunters. But your true place is in the choir."

"It's your choir," Kei snapped back, "not mine!"

"Kei," Ahmisha said, her words soft, hushed, "Your voice earned your place."

But Kei barely listened. She was lost in memory, recalling jealous eyes watching her the first time she stood, leaning on her canes, beside her mother at the head of the choir.

"Can the *Singer's* daughter really earn her spot?" She finally whispered, doubt rippling through each word.

"You were invited to join the choir because," Ahmisha paused, "because the Kopri can *hear* you. They *hear* you! Now come, the celebration is beginning." Ahmisha's slender legs unfolded until she stood above Kei, reaching out a hand and offering to assist her daughter to rise from the sand.

But Kei refused. She grabbed her canes and struggled upright, stiff legs trembling beneath her weight. Ahmisha said nothing. The older woman turned and walked to her place at the head of the choir.

Kei glanced toward her father, who stood by the summoning drum, smoke once more clouding his eyes.

She need only drag her legs across the beach to take her place beside her mother. She need only face the jealous stares of women with voices too low for the Kopri to hear.

But Kei turned away, those jealous stares burning into her back. She struggled to her kayak as her mother's voice rose in a single oscillating note, beginning the assembly.

Her father struck the thick leather head of the summoning drum. Kei leaned into her canes at the edge of the water, feeling its pounding rhythm.

Boom-BOOM. Boom-BOOM. The summoning drum called, sending vibrations through the water.

A hundred Kopri swam nearer to the beach, yellow-tinted tentacles weaving an intricate dance in time with the vibrations pulsing from her father's drum.

Blood pounded in Kei's ears as she flopped onto her kayak, pushing it off the sand. Quick strokes carried her out of the bay, leaving the soaring voices of the choir behind.

* * *

Kei paddled south along the coast, where a dense mangrove forest grew, roots floating out over the water. A long barrier reef lay to the east, protecting the shores from pummeling waves. After twenty minutes, she reached the moonlit channel leading to her father's hut.

Entering his secluded cove, she beached her kayak. She crawled onto the rasping sand and sat alone in the night, facing black water. Dim white moonlight cast shadows on the knotted muscles of her legs. Her hands clenched, and she struck her fists against uncaring thighs.

With only her own voice to keep her company, Kei sang, lips wide and trembling, as she sent her heart's pain echoing over the sea.

Do you see me as I am?
  Swimming deep beneath the waves.
If you see me as I am,
  I will love you all my days.

Her melody rose and fell, but she was alone on the beach, and no one heard her words as she sang:

And I would always see you,
  No matter close or far.
And no matter what the tide brings,
  I will love you as you are.

Tears fell as she sang, and when her last verse faded into the night, she cried while sitting alone on the beach.

Then her voice trailed off as a dark shadow loomed from the water, rising upward until a glowing kopri mantle, covered in pink, burst above the waves. It was OldFish, flashing sad blue harmony with Kei's song.

"*Sorrow,*" Kei's best friend signed tenderly, "*Great sorrow.*"

Kei leaned into the water, cradling the tip of one night-blue tentacle, which hugged her hand in return.

"*Great sorrow,*" OldFish repeated sadly.

"Its not your fault," Kei sang back, keeping her voice pitched high for her oldest friend to hear.

For a moment, the two friends struggled with memories of a raging storm, pummeling a floundering family kayak. Then came the giant wave, overturning the boat and dumping Kei onto a jagged reef. Kei felt that wave again, smashing her into the coral—and the sharp pain along her spine. Then came the numbness where her legs had been, followed by the fragmented memory of her parents being swept away by the currents. And then, the child, Kei, lying battered on the coral, her back bent and broken—until OldFish's questing tentacles pulled her from death's grasp.

"*I found you too late.*" Blue patterns rose and fell around OldFish's eyes.

"But I lived," Kei sang, "because of you."

She tightened her grip on OldFish's tentacle as tremors passed through them both.

"*Great sorrow,*" OldFish signed, their mantle turning from blue to black, their skin painted in dark, patternless despair.

Crystal water lapped against Kei's corded legs. OldFish's rubber-hard tentacle squeezed her fingers once before slipping back beneath the waves, leaving only one eye and one ear knob above the surface.

OldFish pushed sadness into the sea, mantle flashing in dark colors. Kei forgot self-pity as she read her friend's thoughts, shaped on chameleon skin in swirling ridges of green and blue and red.

"*Sister,*" OldFish signed urgently, "*You must return to Tirahanko Bay.*"

"No!" Kei replied, feeling her traitor legs spasm on the chill sand, bitterness filling her voice, "Just leave me alone."

"*Kei, you must come.*"

"I don't want to. The choir doesn't need me."

Silence rose between the two friends, until OldFish finally replied, frustration etched in black lines around their eyes, "*The choir doesn't ask. I do.*"

Kei focused on the rippling, glowing body of the kopri who had saved her life. Her friend, who never asked for anything, but whose mantle now turned jet-black with fear as they signed:

"*A Prophet of the Deep has come, speaking words of doom for all the Kopri. But the Prophet can hear no one in the choir. Not even your mother. You must come!.*" Colors settled into melancholy blue on OldFish's mantle. "*I fear what the Prophet might ask of you, but you must go where currents lead.*"

* * *

Kei had left the safety of her secluded cove and traveled back to Tirahanko with OldFish. Now she bobbed on water at the mouth of the Bay, dreading her return to the ebony beach where the Choir waited.

"Why me?" She complained to her friend, "My voice is nothing special."

"*Oh Kei, I wish you could hear your song. The way we do!*" Pride edged OldFish's emphatic signs. "*If the Prophet can hear anyone, they'll hear you.*"

"My voice isn't that different."

"*It is to our ears. Now hurry. The Prophet waits.*"

OldFish snaked a tentacle around the bow of Kei's kayak, towing her into the bay. The faces of every person Kei knew—human villagers and their allies—turned toward her. In the moonlight, no one noticed the flush rising on her cheeks, nor the slight tremble of her hands. Torches flared, their flames reflecting in the eyes of a hundred kopri drifting in the sheltered waters. Utter silence gripped the bay, which was normally filled with pounding drumbeats and high-pitched songs, celebrating friendship between humans and kopri.

Towed by OldFish, Kei's kayak slipped toward a rock jetty extending from the beach. At the tip of the jetty a wooden structure rose—the Singer's Platform—where the Choir's leader would sing to the Kopri whenever decisions were needed.

Kei's mother, Ahmisha, stood there now, her face lit by torchlight, her voice silent and waiting—refusing to meet Kei's eyes.

When the kayak reached the wooden platform, Kei set her canes on the raised deck. Reaching up, she levered her body onto the wooden planks, flipping to a seated position with a practiced twist.

Her mother waited as Kei took up her canes and struggled to her feet. Then Ahmisha spoke, her words flat and without emotion.

"I know you think your place in my Choir wasn't earned."

Kei said nothing. Her eyes locked onto her mother's shadowed brows.

"You're wrong. Your voice is higher. Clearer than any other. Tonight, Kei, whatever you think of me. You must sing." Ahmisha turned her head, unable to face Kei any longer as jealousy crept into her voice: "it's the kopri who ask. Not me."

Kei's fingers tightened on the handles of her canes, breath freezing in her chest. Her gaze traveled across the water, over the waiting eyes and ear knobs of the assembled kopri. And further north, to where the drummers waited motionless above the surf. Her father stood there, face glowing in torchlight. His head tilted, returning her stare. Smiling with eyes that for once seemed undimmed.

And on the beach, behind the jetty — the singers of the Choir. All silent.

Waiting.

"The kopri have spoken," Amisha said, her voice falling flat into the night, "one of their wise ones, *DeepRunner,* has come from beyond the Aguerda — the mangrove swamp that separates our inland Nadako Sea from the great outer ocean."

"Why haven't you sung?" Kei asked, genuinely confused. Her mother's voice was high and pure: there was a reason she was the leader of the choir!

"I tried, daughter," Amisha replied, a sense of failure running bitter through her words. "We all did. But DeepRunner is ancient and cannot hear us."

"What makes you think the Prophet will hear my song?"

"The kopri believe you will be heard." Her mother's upper lip trembled, then her shoulders slumped and she turned away, walking across the jetty and joining her silent choir.

Kei's eyes lingered on her mother, then she turned to look out over the bay, knuckles whitening as she gripped her canes. A rippling bulge moved through the water toward Kei. Two enormous kopri eyes broke the surface of the waves, head rising, exposing ear knobs to the air. Torches on the platform flickered as phosphorescent signs — formed of bumps and grooves and colors — swept over the ancient prophet's mantle.

"*Sing child!*" DeepRunner signed, "*I must hear you before I speak.*" A long scar cut the flesh beneath their eyes, a bitter reminder of the past. DeepRunner floated beside the platform, silent and waiting.

Kei trembled, shivers running along her arms. Notes froze in her chest, which ceased movement. Then her father's hands struck his drum — *Bum-boom! Bum-boom!* — and Kei remembered to breathe. Her father's heartbeat rhythms cleared her thoughts. Words of greeting bubbled into her mind. Her voice rose, sweet dulcet tones piercing into the star-filled sky.

"*Rise now, new light,*" Kei sang, forgetting the tightness of her legs as her angelic voice soared above the bay, "*And swim with me, within the current. I greet you. My friend from below.*" Her last tone faded, a brief echo shimmering across the water.

The choir held its breath. Her father's drumming hands fell silent. Kopri mantles stayed dark and smooth, enormous eyes focused on the ancient prophet floating beneath Kei.

"I hear you, Singer," the ancient kopri flashed, word-signs glowing in bumps and ridges beneath their scar. *"From beneath the waves, I greet my friend above."*

Kei stared into glowing eyes, uncertain of what to say, but then DeepRunner flashed green, mantle rising into the air, signs brightening and throbbing as the ancient Prophet spoke.

"Singer." DeepRunner signed. *"Friend above the waves. The humans of the Floating Islands have invaded our spawning grounds. They shatter our nests and steal our food, leaving nothing behind."*

As the prophet signed, the long scar beneath their eyes pulsed red with remembered loss and pain.

"Since they have come, our numbers dwindle. What younglings manage to survive starve, and their minds no longer light with thought. These invaders sing no words. They read no signs. Like beasts, their skin is mute." DeepRunner's mantle dimmed to a silent grey, as the old kopri sought their next words carefully.

"Singer!" DeepRunner finally shouted out, signs flashing rapidly, bright and urgent. *"Ride the currents with me! Sing my words to these humans on their floating islands. Translate for me. Tell them to leave our spawning grounds untouched."*

The ancient kopri surged from the water, whirling tentacles pushing them into the air as words pulsed bright on their mantle: urgent, demanding, and pleading.

"Join me, Singer! Help me restore our spawning grounds, so my children's children may hunt with yours. Join me, singer: you are my final hope."

With a last flash of rippling blue sadness, DeepRunner sank, eyes closing, disappearing into the depths.

All was still and silent in the bay, until OldFish slowly emerged, rising above the water, mantle turquoise and tinged with black. Rippling signs swept across OldFish, who spoke with phosphorescent color, visible both above and below the waves.

"*Tomorrow night,*" OldFish signed reluctantly to Kei, "*The Prophet will return to hear your decision.*"

Then OldFish, too, sank beneath the waves. And silence reigned in Tirahanko Bay.

Sister of My Heart

OldFish lurked within a yellow coral tree that thrust spiky branches from the reef. One hooded eye tracked a spiny lobster spidering toward OldFish's camouflaged hiding spot. The lobster paused, poised to strike at an unsuspecting shrimp. OldFish watched the lobster. The lobster watched the shrimp. Suddenly, the thorny branch of a nearby coral twisted into the gray-black tentacle of DeepRunner, the tentacle's camouflaged form dissolving in a lightning-fast strike toward the lobster.

But DeepRunner had struck too soon—and missed. The spiny lobster skittered away, darting backward straight into OldFish's waiting tentacles. Tooth-edged suckers clamped down, and with a snap of OldFish's hardened beak, the crustacean cracked in half. The kopri's ribboned tongue, lined with hundreds of tiny razor-sharp teeth, rasped over the still-living flesh, tearing it apart in greedy bites.

"Patience," OldFish signed, mantle sparkling in rainbow-hued amusement.

"I would have taken it!" DeepRunner replied defensively, *"but, you were in the way!"*

"Maybe," OldFish laughed, *"but the prey is in my beak, not yours."*

DeepRunner's mantle flared darkest red, but they flashed no further signs, their enormous eyes simply staring while OldFish ate the kill.

With the lobster devoured and its head and shell discarded to the microbes on the ocean floor, OldFish pulled closer to DeepRunner, tentacle tips gently brushing the ancient kopri's mantle.

"She is broken," OldFish said sadly. *"Do you understand this?"*

"Who is broken?" DeepRunner asked, pulling away from OldFish's gentle touch.

"The singer. Kei. The only human you can hear."

"Broken?" Deep Runner said, surprised, *"But its voice echoes through my ears."*

"Her voice, yes." OldFish replied, *"But she is still broken."*

"How?" DeepRunner asked, confused, *"They all look the same to me. There's so many of them, humans, like sand crabs skittering on the beach."*

OldFish stared at the older kopri, patience rippling through their words, *"Humans walk on land, like that lobster crawled on the seafloor. But Kei's legs are damaged. They are like ancient coral, strong enough to bear weight, but hardened and unmoving."*

When OldFish signed Kei's name, yellow and orange dots swirled in magenta rings, surrounded by a pink haze of love.

"*No matter,*" DeepRunner's mantle shifted colors, settling into a dismissive dull brown. "*The human has its kayak. Its arms are strong. I will help it swim against the currents. I need the human to sing to the floating islands. Make them understand.*"

"*It will be perilous for Kei, alone above the waves,*" OldFish signed, their skin rippling uneasily, like the turbulent surface of the ocean.

"*It will do as its told!*" DeepRunner nearly shouted, anger bubbling just beneath the surface of their words, "*Humans are tools — good for nets, hunts, and little else. They are NOT people!*"

"*How are they different than us?*" OldFish quickly challenged, "*We hunt together. We nest together. And they can glow pink with love, like us.*"

"*But they don't breathe the ocean's tides,*" DeepRunner snapped back, "*They don't build their nests in the spawning grounds, out in the vastness of the ocean. They hide here in their shallow bays. They are NOT kopri.*"

Gray washed over OldFish's mantle, tentacles releasing their light touch on DeepRunner. The smaller kopri remained silent, unwilling to contradict the ancient Prophet from the Deep — no matter how wrong DeepRunner was. Instead, wrinkles formed around OldFish's eyes, pulsing black with worry.

"*I fear for her,*" OldFish signed, "*with her damaged legs.*"

"*I don't care about your fear. Or its broken tentacles. What is the life of one human animal when our children are threatened?*"

DeepRunner flared phosphorescent red, the ragged scar beneath their eyes throbbing and angry, challenging OldFish, who asked, *"Are the humans of the floating islands really that dangerous?"*

Teal shades of blue-green curiosity flickered around OldFish's questioning eyes, as DeepRunner replied, *"Their islands float across the spawn beds, dragging chains to break the reefs."* The scar on the older kopri's face throbbed a dark blue, sad memories washing over their skin as they continued speaking, *"their humans lower nets bigger than a storm, dragging younglings above the waves. They take all the food, all the leafpeople floating on the surface. Leaving our younglings starving. And the young that survive the nets are signless, living alone like animals."*

With that, DeepRunner's mantle faded to a silent grey and no words passed between the two for some time, until OldFish finally replied, *"I have not been to the outer sea since I first awakened."* A bewildered orange slowly formed on OldFish's mantle as an unexpected question poured forth, *"Why are the younglings speechless?"*

DeepRunner didn't answer, staying silent grey for a moment. But then anger and frustration bubbled up into their reply, *"I don't know! Everything has changed! The spawning beds are barren and broken. The leafpeople the younglings eat are gone. Everything is changed. Our world is dead!"*

Mournfulness haunted DeepRunner's eyes, great sadness filling their words, *"I must speak to the humans of the floating islands. Make them stop!"*

"*And what of Kei?*" OldFish flashed back, "*will she be safe?*"

Bright red thorns spiked along DeepRunner's mantle. "*If you are afraid for your pet, then swim the currents with me and protect it. But I will take your human with me, broken or not. So it can sing to the floating islands. So I can order them to stop.*"

"*And if they don't?*"

"*They must,*" DeepRunner signed, the scar livid below their eyes, "*I will not have another chance.*"

DeepRunner flashed once, then faded to inky black, jetting away and refusing to read OldFish's worried sign.

* * *

Kei sat with her back to the morning sunlight, which streamed over the damp sands of Tirahanko Bay, still slick from the retreating tide. To the west, a dense green jungle carpeted the slopes of Mt. Jikea. The eldest villagers claimed that rivers of flame once flowed through lava tubes and emptied into the sea, but the dry tunnels had long since cooled, and the villagers used them to store preserved food.

The harvest continued this morning, with villagers casting their nets to catch the last fish still trapped in the bay. Other villagers used sharp flint knives to cut fillets, placing them on racks to dry in the sun.

Kei's people wasted no part of the fish. Beyond food, they cleaned, tanned, and stitched lengths of fish skin into thin, crinkled leather. The villagers used the fish guts as fertilizer for their gardens and fields, while boiling the bones into a thick stew, seasoned with peppercorns and fragrant tubers.

This morning, Kei sat with the elders, weaving palm leaf baskets to store preserved fish in the dry, cool depths of the lava tunnels. Her kayak was unnecessary today, and the other harvest tasks required sturdy legs. The ancient aunties and uncles welcomed her with warm smiles, making a space for her in their weaving circle. Still, she felt like a child, given pretend work to make her feel useful.

One aged auntie, sister-in-law to Kei's great-grandmother, peered at Kei from beneath sparse gray hair.

"Your decisions are your own," the old woman said, her fingers moving deftly through the palm fronds.

Kei frowned, her gaze fixed on her father, busy at the north end of the beach working on her kayak. From this distance, she couldn't make out what he was doing, but at least he was up and working. Not lying in the smoky stupor he'd been in for weeks.

"I know," Kei replied, her voice tight.

"Do you?" The auntie's voice was low, but it held a weight Kei could feel.

Kei said nothing, keeping her eyes on her father. The silence hung between them, then she shook her head and turned to face the old woman.

"I don't know what I'm going to do. My mother doesn't want me to go with the Kopri."

"No parent wants their child to leave home."

Kei lifted her eyes, meeting the auntie's gaze, saying, "My father doesn't care."

"He doesn't need to," the auntie replied. "Your choice is your own."

"My mother says it's too dangerous."

"Every mother says that."

Kei hesitated, fingers curling in the fronds. "My legs—" she started to say.

But it wasn't her legs that filled her thoughts. It was her mother's face, strained and sad. And afraid.

The auntie's voice interrupted the silent ache. "Your legs aren't needed in a kayak," she said, as though finishing Kei's unspoken words.

"That's what I told her. But... she's right. It's dangerous."

"Child," the old woman rasped, her breath shaky in the warm air, "life is dangerous. But—you could always stay here. Weaving baskets."

Then the old woman fell silent, her voice dimming as her gnarled fingers struggled with the palm strands. Kei's own hands were still smooth, young, and strong. She could feel the tension in her joints, the restless energy in her fingers. But what if this was all she was meant to do? Weave baskets and stay safe—until the years pulled her body down, until her hands swelled and her skin wrinkled, until her mind dimmed with age.

Either way—she would die.

A small laugh escaped Kei's lips. Auntie was right: life was dangerous! But fear was worse. And Kei was tired of the way her heart clenched every time she thought of the long years ahead, of her legs growing stiffer with age while other people's children grew into adults.

Putting down her basket, Kei picked up her canes and pushed herself to her feet, leaving behind long drag marks in the sand as she struggled toward her father and her kayak — and whatever adventure awaited now that she'd made her choice.

* * *

Two nights had passed since DeepRunner asked for Kei's help. Morning sun broke through the reed curtains covering the door and windows of her father's hut, casting shadows on his unconscious face. Puffed skin under his eyes held the gray hue of smoke, and his breath wheezed, droning in the dim light. The day before, he had added outriggers to Kei's kayak, attaching hollowed logs to each side with long, flexible poles. The sealed logs would float on the ocean's surface, giving the kayak stability and preventing it from tipping over.

Her father had also woven tow ropes into the bow — for kopri tentacles to grip — and secured waterskins and dried fruit to the frame.

But he had not said goodbye. Instead, they argued before Kei left to accept DeepRunner's invitation. He had stared at her stiffened legs, and she had grown angry, leaving him behind with his guilt. Later that night, she returned from Tirahanko Bay to find her kayak ready, but her father senseless, wrapped in white fumes that curled untended from his still lit pipe.

She had planned to leave this morning with the turning tide, hoping to say goodbye to her father without anger. But he had burned that chance away in his pipe bowl. She stared at his indifference, the acrid scent of smoke lingering in the air, a sharp reminder of words unsaid.

A rustling caught Kei's attention. She turned as the door curtain parted and her mother, Ahmisha, stepped through. Ahmisha's disapproving eyes took in the hut's clutter, nose wrinkling at the stench of the pipe. Her gaze rested on her husband, snoring on his grass pallet on the floor.

"Nothing's changed, I see," Ahmisha said. Kei followed her mother's eyes to her father's face. The first wrinkles of middle age had marked the years there, matching the wrinkles around Ahmisha's eyes.

"He got my kayak ready," Kei said, "he built outriggers."

Ahmisha's lips turned down sourly as she reply, "I saw. I checked his knots before coming in. Sturdy enough. He at least can still do that."

Outside the hut, parrots called from the high branches of palm trees, while a sighing breeze whispered across the cove.

"He talked to OldFish about the tow ropes," Kei said. "OldFish and DeepRunner agreed to pull me. It will be faster than just paddling."

"OldFish—" Ahmisha's voice dropped away as sadness filled her eyes. "You aren't responsible for the Kopri. They have no right to ask." As she spoke, Ahmisha reached out one trembling hand, placing it on Kei's shoulder. "You don't have to do this."

"DeepRunner says there'll be no more kopri younglings if I don't," Kei said, locking her eyes on her mother's, her voice filling with regret. "There will only be speechless kopri, living alone. Just solitary animals, like any other octopus in the sea."

"The Kopri aren't people!" Ahmisha said, "Not like us!"

"Aren't they?" Kei replied, "Without them, who would we sing too? Who would fill our nets during the hunt? Without our friends, you would just be a weaver, not the leader of the Choir."

Kei paused, reached up and took her mother's hand in her own, "And without the Kopri, I would have died when I was nine years old. On the barrier reef. OldFish would not have been there to pull me to safety." Ahmisha glanced at Kei's legs, eyes wincing in memory.

"No, mother, I don't have to go. But I owe the Kopri my life. How can I say no?"

"You owe no one anything. You didn't ask to be on that kayak in rough seas. Your father and I put you there. And OldFish chose to save you, despite the danger." Ahmisha looked away from Kei, toward her sleeping husband. "You don't owe your father either."

"He thinks it was his fault," Kei said. "I see it every time he looks at my legs."

"Don't walk that path with him!" Anger tinged Ahmisha's voice. "No one saw the storm coming. Not him. Not me. Not the Kopri. Squalls happen."

"Squalls happen," Kei repeated. "But I'm the one who bears the scars."

"You do," Kei's mother replied.

"I'm useless here. I can't even climb the NetSinger's platform without someone else hanging the rope!"

"But your singing!" Ahmisha said, pride ringing through her words. But Kei didn't hear the anguish in her mother's voice, or hear her mother's love.

Instead, Kei shouted bitterly, "My voice is NOT enough! It's not enough! I'll always be *the cripple*. I hear it every day! I'm just the Singer's crippled daughter!"

Kei's father snored gently as Ahmisha and Kei locked eyes, but Ahmisha stayed silent. The truth in Kei's words came between them — and words spoken could not be unsaid.

Kei gripped her canes, tearing her eyes from her mother. Then she turned and left her father's hut, dragging her anger across the sand. Leaving both her parents behind.

The kopri — and her destiny — waited for her.

Dead Water

Kei paddled away from Tirahanko, fighting the pull of the rising tide. On the far horizon, whitecaps foamed over the outer barrier reef that guarded the coast. She followed OldFish and DeepRunner, who navigated channels twisting through submerged hummocks spreading as far as Kei could see. A shiver ran along her spine in memory of the hard corals of that churning barrier reef, years ago.

Crashing booms echoed over the water as Kei paddled closer to the reef. With each stroke, her stomach twisted tighter, refusing to release. But the tide was shifting, slowly swallowing the reef's jagged corals. The tide heights meant little to OldFish and DeepRunner, who could glide effortlessly through the reef's submerged canyons. But Kei's kayak could only pass safely at high tide — and even then, the swelling waves barely concealed the jagged rocks.

As she approached, her ears throbbed, a cold sweat covering her forehead despite the warm sun beating down. OldFish rose then to the surface, mantle rippling.

"The way is clear, Kei," OldFish signed. *"Put up your paddle, we will tow you over."*

Kei clenched the hand grips of her paddle, reluctant to relinquish control of the kayak. But OldFish and DeepRunner extended their fluid tentacles from the sea, gripping the ropes fastened to the vessel's bow. With a powerful contraction of their mantles, they jetted forward, pulling the small boat behind them. Kei's breath came in rapid gasps, but she set aside her paddle, tying it securely to the side.

And then she watched. And waited. The ocean swelled before her, relentless, as the tide surged over the reef. Her fingers dug into the reed sides of her boat, clenching, knuckles whitening with fear. A lump rose in her throat, her stomach twisting as the reef loomed closer. She couldn't breathe. Her mind flooded with the memory of her last crossing—when a sudden squall had driven her family's sea kayak off course. Not far from here, she had struck the coral, her spine snapping as saltwater burned her lungs.

But then that memory was swept away by a mountainous wave, crashing over her as OldFish and DeepRunner hauled her kayak up and over the reef. Together, they surged over the towering peak, then plummeted down the other side. As they skimmed dangerously close to the jagged corals of the barrier reef, Kei's heart skipped a beat, and the memory of ancient pain flared along her spine. But then the two kopri gave a final burst of power, propelling her into the open waters of the Nadako Sea, leaving the safety of her home behind.

* * *

Hours after crossing over the barrier reef, there was no land in sight. A heavy stillness settled over the sea as she paddled toward Anziko, an island midway between Tirahanko and the Aguerda—the vast mangrove swamp that separated the inner and outer seas. Anziko was a large, populated island with a safe harbor where Kei could rest and replenish her supply of freshwater. But it was also the last place Kei had walked and danced before the unexpected storm pushed her family's kayak into the reefs.

Amid the endless swells, whitecaps flecked the water. Coral columns rose to the surface, sometimes forming small reef-protected islets that broke the larger waves, leaving the surface of the Nadako calm. Kei's kayak skimmed over the water, towed by her kopri companions.

"It's strange," Kei said to OldFish, breaking the eerie silence during a moment of rest. "We've traveled less than a day, but this is a different world."

"You and I were here before," OldFish replied.

"I know. But I was a child. My parents were my entire world then. This is different."

"The water tastes the same to me as the last time we were here," OldFish signed.

Kei smiled, shaking her head, "there is more to the world than salt in your beak," she said, laughing. "Don't you remember your parents?"

"Kopri lives are different from humans," OldFish replied. *"Once I left the spawning grounds, I never saw my parents again."*

"Doesn't that make you sad?"

"No," OldFish replied, *"we are not like you. Once we join a hunting pod, that becomes our family."*

Kei considered OldFish's answer for moment, lost in her own memories, then said thoughtfully, "When we paddled beyond Tirahanko's barrier reef seven years ago, I remember feeling safe, sitting behind my father. Now I'm alone—" She paused, her gaze drifting over the waves, a frown tugging at her lips. For a moment, the ocean closed in around her, but then a grin spread across her upturned lips, and light danced in her eyes. "It's scary. But I'm free. I mean—it's just me. And what I'm doing matters. More than anything I've ever done before!"

"But you have me!" OldFish laughed, mantle sparkling in rainbow amusement as they raised a yellow-pulsing tentacle tip above the water and *thwacked* it back down, splashing Kei's burnished skin with drops of brine. Kei grinned, striking the water and splashing OldFish in return.

"It's not fair," Kei sang, sputtering. "You live in the water! And you know what I mean! I'm on my own. Without my parents."

Thwack went OldFish's tentacle again, and for a moment, the two friends laughed and forgot about the daunting journey ahead of them.

"OldFish," Kei sang, her cadence growing serious once again. "Are you sure we're heading toward my aunt's island? How do you find your way? It's just water as far as I can see. It all looks the same."

OldFish's tentacles hung lithe in the water, then flexed like unwinding snakes, pushing an ear knob above the surface. Blue-green thoughtfulness etched OldFish's puckering signs.

"You feel the direction of the wind. I sense the ebb of currents," OldFish explained. *"Menehko, the Great Outer Ocean, sends its tides through the mangrove swamps your people call the Aguerda — the barrier that separates the inner and outer seas. Most of the Aguerda is too shallow to swim through, but a few wide channels cut through the mangrove roots. I feel Menehko's current, its endless cycle that encircles the world. Sometimes it pushes, sometimes it pulls. But the tides of Menehko are the beginning and the end of all currents in the world. Its vibrations guide me, allowing me to find my way."*

"Like the sea breeze that told us the storm was coming. Before the wreck." Kei said. A knot tightened in her stomach, stirred by memories awakened during her recent crossing of the enormous barrier reef—the same reef where the childhood wreck had claimed her legs. OldFish's mantle remained smooth and gray, silent and unreadable—until, slowly, mottled blue swirled across its surface, edging it with sadness.

Time passed. Waves rose and fell. The companions drifted on in silence.

"The swells are smaller now," Kei sang as her two kopri companions floated at rest, their tentacles stretching languidly across the ocean's placid surface. "I remember waves as high as palm trees."

OldFish turned one eye on Kei, adding, *"That night was a bright moon. Waves always climb higher when the moon shines full. And – the storm was coming."*

"The storm." Kei frowned, rubbing a hardened muscle in her upper thigh. "I remember wind. Dark skies sweeping over the moon."

"Your father paddled hard to reach your home before the storm arrived."

"We all paddled," Kei said. "The storm came from nowhere."

"Such is the way of storms, for you humans above water."

Kei nodded, then continued, "I remember endless swells. White spume surging over the reef. Father yelling as the current dragged us into the rocks." Then her song faded, lost in the memory of storm waves slamming her family's sea kayak against the reef, its bundled reeds shattering on the unforgiving coral.

"Swim the currents you are in, Kei," OldFish signed gently. *"You can't swim in tides that rose before."*

"Stop talking about the past, you mean," Kei replied.

Rippling green flashed agreement across the kopri's mantle. But before Kei could reply, DeepRunner pushed a throbbing mantle above the sea, signing brightly in knobs tipped with black, demanding the others' attention.

"*I smell your dead water,*" the larger kopri signed bluntly, "*the stink of it is near.*"

"Fresh water, you mean," Kei sang, laughing. "Flowing into the sea from streams on my aunt's island."

"*Saltless!*" DeepRunner flashed, black and gray with annoyance, "*Saltless water, not fit for people. Deadwater.*"

Kei laughed again, taking up her paddle. "For you maybe," Kei replied, "but my people need fresh water."

Her two companions slipped tentacles around the knotted tow ropes, mantles contracting, jetting through waves with the kayak racing behind them. Kei pushed her lips together and dug her paddle into the sea. Land was near! Her breathing steadied and her clenched stomach loosened with the thought of beaching her kayak on sand.

Kei's lips curled into a broad smile. For the first time on the journey, she lost herself in the joy of speed and the strain of her muscles, forgetting for a moment that she was nearing her aunt's village, the last place she had visited with her family before the reef had stolen her legs. Together, the kopri and the girl skimmed the kayak over the water, moving faster than any human could alone.

Fiery red clouds glowed behind her as Kei's kayak glided over a stretch of vibrant coral gardens, which shielded her aunt's island from storm waves. Water, clear as glass, sparkled with all the colors of the rainbow, painted on fronds and branches and mounds growing beneath the surface. A thousand tiny fish flickered through the garden, flashing yellow, red, green and blue.

With a few more strokes of Kei's paddle, the group passed over the coral gardens and entered the smooth waters of a bay, where the village rose above a yellow sand beach. This bay had no hot spring pools or high cliffs, but knobs of old coral rose along its sides, allowing the villagers to string nets across the mouth of the bay, trapping prey. On one old coral growth, a NetSinger's Platform perched above the water. Low enough, Kei thought, that she would need no rope to climb it.

Several kopri floated in the bay's open waters, flashing greeting signs to OldFish and DeepRunner as they towed Kei's kayak to the beach. Further back from shore, mangrove forests receded toward the unseen center of the island. Huts and long houses stood in a clearing carved into the thick jungle growth, near tidy vegetable gardens bordered by trees heavy with sweet-scented fruit.

As the bow of Kei's kayak crunched onto yellow sand, dozens of villagers approached, led by a middle-aged woman who sang greetings to both Kei and the kopri. The Singer's melody rang high and sweet across the water. Kei heard her mother's voice in the woman's sweet notes and saw her mother's eyes gazing back at her across the sand. Vague memories stirred from her last visit here, seven years ago. Kei recognized her aunt, her mother's sister, who sang a welcome song to them:

Welcome travelers,
Welcome Friends,
Welcome to our island.
Rest along our shore
While we prepare the feast.
Welcome to our island
Where you may sleep, in peace.

OldFish pushed an ear above the water, listening to the welcoming lyrics, and signing a crinkled brown greeting in return. But DeepRunner, who could hear no human but Kei, stayed beneath the waves, mantle flat and gray.

Kei thrust her paddle into lapping water and pushed her kayak forward, beaching it on the yellow sand. Waning sunlight deepened the red in Kei's flushed cheeks as she gripped her unresponsive legs and lifted them over the edge of her kayak, guiding them into the water with practiced hands.

Neither her aunt, nor the other villagers, said anything as Kei untied her canes and struggled to her feet. She moistened dry lips, cleared her throat, and lifted her voice in the greeting song's response:

Thank you Friends,
For the blessing of your shore,

Thank you Friends,
For we can swim no more,

In gratitude, we rest with you,
And pause upon our way,
Thank you, friends, oh thank you,
For the blessings of your shore.

Each word rang with pure, crisp tones, which brought smiles to every villager on the beach. And behind her, rainbow flashes flickered through the bay, kopri laughter silent on the waves.

Kei's aunt stepped forward, embracing her. "Welcome, niece. Welcome to your home," she said, before leading Kei through the crowd of smiling villagers. As Kei moved away from the beach, her gaze swept across villagers wading into the shallows, offering mangoes to their kopri guests, whose tentacles curled in eager acceptance.

Kei followed her aunt toward the Singer's Longhouse, her steps slow and hesitant. Once inside, she set aside her canes and sank gratefully onto a reed mat. The coolness of the mat melted the tension from her limbs as the last rays of sunset bled into the night. Her aunt served her mashed cassava and strips of raw fish; a sharp tang of lemony citrus and the heat of ground peppercorns added zest to the meal. They both drank cool water from gourds, just the two of them, in a thatch-roofed longhouse large enough to hold 20 people at once, lit now by a single flickering torch.

Seven years separated them, but her aunt looked up, head tilting to one side, with a soft smile lighting her face.

"Is your mother still Singer?" the older woman asked.

"She is." Kei replied.

"And your father?"

Kei thought about the drugged confusion dimming her father's eyes and his rasping snores — her only farewell. But she kept that to herself, saying instead, "he sleeps too much, but still plays the summoning drum."

"He always played so well," her aunt said, a nostalgic smile tugging at her lips. "He kept the beat the night I was married." Her aunt's smile faltered, fading as her gaze dropped to Kei's legs. "But you were there," she added, her voice trailing off in embarrassment.

Kei took a sip of water, her mind racing — anger, embarrassment, sadness. The wreck had occurred during her return to Tirahanko after her aunt's wedding, and the memory of that gathering threatened to pull her back into the past. She swallowed, saying, "I remember that night. I danced. And I swam with the Kopri. OldFish was there. And I ate those sweet cakes you made."

"I will make some for you," her aunt said, her smile returning. "But can't you stay longer than just tonight? I would like to sing with you, niece."

Kei looked into her aunt's warm eyes. There was no judgment there. No pity. Her aunt saw her as she was — one Singer to another.

"If it was just me, I would," Kei said, "But DeepRunner is eager to be off. We only stopped here to refill my waterskins."

A frown darkened her aunt's face as the older woman spoke: "DeepRunner stopped here before crossing to your village. I sang as clearly as I could. We all did. But DeepRunner could not hear us. We asked the other kopri to translate for us, but DeepRunner said no. That one has too much pride, from swimming for so long alone in the Deep."

"DeepRunner acts like I'm their servant." Kei said, agreeing.

"I suppose we are," her aunt replied. "We help them during hunts. Close the nets and let them eat first. So I suppose we are servants of the Kopri. But don't they serve us too? Thanks to the Kopri, we always have fish. No one in any village of the Nadako knows hunger. So are we their servants? Or are they ours?"

Kei's brows tightened, her eyes thoughtful. "OldFish is just my friend," she said. "I don't like the way DeepRunner flashes commands at me, but the survival of the Kopri is at stake."

Her aunt nodded, her smile dropping into a sigh as she spoke. "And so you are going through the Aguerda, out into the Deep."

"Someone must speak for DeepRunner!" Kei said, her voice firm.

Her aunt stared at Kei, eyes questioning as she spoke, "You intend to speak to the people of the floating islands — the Koru-Kah?"

"Yes. The Koru-Kah," Kei confirmed, her voice steady.

"They are little more than beasts themselves," her aunt replied, "or so it seems to me. Our kopri allies say the Koru-Kah have no language. They can't read sign. And they speak no words that kopri can hear."

Kei replied quickly, "But they are people. Human, like us."

"Human, but *not* like us." Her aunt's voice dropped into silence, darkness filling troubled eyes. "Kei, you need to know. Others have gone with DeepRunner before. Twenty years ago, a Singer from the Meransi Islands visited us here on Anziko, on her way to the outer ocean with DeepRunner. She never returned. The kopri said the Koru-Kah took her onto the floating islands, but they never heard her song again."

Kei's eyes widened, but she remained silent.

"You didn't know?" Her aunt asked, voice melting into the air between them.

Kei shook her head from side to side, closing her eyes and trying to stay calm.

"And now DeepRunner returns," her aunt said, eyes narrowing as she spoke, "Asking for another Singer, showing no regret for the one who was lost. And how many others have they taken over those years?" Her aunt paused, anger flickering in her eyes: "Kei, you can't go!"

"And if I don't? Do you think it's true? That the Kopri will disappear?"

Kei's aunt pressed her lips into a hard white line, and when she spoke, her words cut reluctantly through the air: "Our kopri friends, our hunting partners. They say this is true. Fewer younglings come from Menehko each year. This season, none arrived. I don't know if the reason is the Koru-Kah. But yes, the Kopri are disappearing from the Nadako Sea."

"Then what choice do I have?" Kei asked, frustration rising in her voice. "What happens if we don't help our friends? I don't care about DeepRunner. But the others. Do we only help our friends when the fishing is easy?"

"A bundle of sticks," her aunt said, her voice quiet but firm.

"What?" Kei asked, furrowing her brow.

Her aunt smiled faintly. "The children's story. The one about the bundle of sticks."

Kei's confusion deepened. "I don't understand."

Her aunt's gaze softened as she spoke, "When we're alone, we're vulnerable, like a single stick. Easily broken. But when we stand together, bound as one, we're unbreakable. That's how humans and kopri have survived. Together, we're stronger."

Kei sat still, the words sinking deep within her, their meaning slowly unfurling. "One stick," she murmured, "one stick, by itself, will break like I did. Alone on the coral."

"But together…" her aunt prodded gently, until Kei replied, "Together, a bundle of sticks will not break. Without OldFish pulling me from the reef, I would have died."

The longhouse fell into a deep silence as Kei reflected on her aunt's words, her own vulnerability, and the strength that could come from working together. Her father's face flashed in her mind—both the drugged detachment she had seen and the warmth she remembered. Despite it all, he had been a large part of her life, along with her friends and family, keeping her safe.

"Well then," Kei said, pushing away her longing for home, "what choice do I have? And I won't be going there alone. There'll be three of us. Three sticks. I'll have OldFish and DeepRunner with me, keeping me safe."

"What do you mean?" Her aunt asked.

"DeepRunner says we'll approach the Koru-Kah's large hunting kayaks when they leave their floating islands. With OldFish and DeepRunner towing me away, no one can catch me if things go wrong."

The current before Kei was unavoidable, and she could not turn aside, no matter how much she wanted to. Her stomach clenched, but she expanded her chest, then released air slowly, relaxing the muscles of her throat. A comforting ritual, preparing her voice for song.

She continued breathing until her voice was ready. Instead of tears falling, Kei sent a melody soaring through the longhouse. Her aunt joined in, and for the rest of the evening, the pair spoke in a language shared only by musicians. Harmony and rhythm, voices entwining, becoming one shared note filling their world with song.

And in the morning, her aunt fulfilled her promise, sending Kei off on her journey with sweet cakes, wrapped in cured fish skins to protect them from the water.

The Aguerda Swamp

After leaving her aunt's island, Kei slept two nights on the open sea. Each night, sleep crept upon her as she lay awake, replaying her aunt's revelation—that another Singer had left with DeepRunner and had never been heard from again. In the emptiness of her days, waves billowed undisturbed in a vast blue expanse. Whenever she looked at the kopri, betrayal stabbed her. Neither OldFish nor DeepRunner had told her of the other Singer lost to the Koru-Kah. She ached, wishing she was home in her father's hut. Or listening to her mother's voice leading the choir in Tirahanko Bay.

Once, she spotted a high-flying albatross, immense wings spread wide and soaring with the wind in a cloudless sky, but otherwise she and the kopri were the only living creatures in view. Whenever DeepRunner flashed an arrogant black, Kei's breath quickened. She left her thoughts unsung and clung to her anger, too afraid to confront the haughty kopri Prophet. She floated silently on the surface of the sea — a mere speck lost in the vastness of the world.

On the third evening, she rested on the sandy shore of a tiny islet that rose from shallow waters near a wide channel leading into the Aguerda swamp. Her canes remained tied to her kayak, unusable on the rough surface of the islet. Instead, she crawled over sand, rock, and fallen palm fronds, scooping up overripe mangoes from beneath stunted trees and tossing them toward the beach. Soft pulp smeared her fingers — but to the Kopri, few land delicacies were more prized than half-rotten mango. The kopri loved mushy fruit that pulped sweetly in their beaks. In gratitude, Old Fish had jetted off to a coral reef, seeking one of the meaty conch snails Kei loved so much. But DeepRunner lingered at the beach's edge, savoring mangoes, oblivious to the effort it took Kei to crawl over the island's uneven ground to gather them.

The ancient kopri's condescension boiled inside Kei, seething like storm-churned waves, swirling with thoughts of the lost Singer. She turned to confront DeepRunner.

"I read your sign, you know," Kei sang, tossing more fruit into the water. Heat flushed her cheeks as she lay with her legs stretched achingly into the surf, but she could no longer contain her anger, "The water is clear enough for me to read you," she sang, "even at the end of the tow rope."

DeepRunner rolled one fist-sized eye toward the beach, ear knob quivering with the vibrations of Kei's voice. A ring of alternating orange and turquoise bumps formed around DeepRunner's eyes—questioning, demanding an explanation. Kei's voice rose to its highest notes, maintaining harmony and rhythm as her sing-song words cut through the air, vibrating sharply against DeepRunner's ear knob.

"I am not your servant!" Kei sang, each word a flashing dagger. "I am your NetSinger. Here above the waves to guide you. And when we reach the Floating Islands, I will sing for you. But I am not your pet. I do not serve you. I am here for the kopri of my hunting pod. Not you."

The ancient kopri pressed coiled tentacles into the sand, raising their mantle to expose ear knobs to the air. Both eyestalks swiveled toward Kei as DeepRunner's mantle turned jet black—demanding obedience.

"I'm not your pet!" Kei repeated.

DeepRunner's smooth black flesh molted into gray knobs, annoyance rippling over silent skin. Kei straightened her back, pushing herself upright with her arms, head held high as she sat erect on the sand.

"You are broken!" DeepRunner flashed, black knobs around eyestalks turning an angry red.

"My kayak still cuts the waves!"

"OldFish says you cannot go to the Koru-Kah. Your lower tentacles are broken."

"Maybe," Kei replied, feeling warm water lap against her stiff legs. "But I don't need them. My voice fills the air. And I WILL sing to the Koru-Kah!"

"But you can't go onto their floating islands."

"Why would I?" Kei asked, bitter anger building in her words, which she threw at DeepRunner, "You said we would greet them when they left their islands on their hunting kayaks. Or were you going to abandon me to the Koru-Kah? Like you did the other Singer before?"

DeepRunner's mantle turned dark red, the scar below their eyes puckering in anger.

Kei hissed through clenched lips, "My Aunt told me! I know what you did!"

As the pair glared at one another, neither noticed a bulging ripple approaching the beach. Water spilled from OldFish's mantle as the smaller kopri pushed up from the gentle surf and dropped an enormous conch snail at Kei's feet. OldFish reached for a mango, then hesitated, glancing first at DeepRunner, then at Kei. Orange and turquoise patterns rippled in questioning ridges around each of OldFish's eyes.

Kei turned to face her friend.

"And when were you going to tell me?" She sang, lowering her pitch so that only OldFish could hear her anger.

"*Tell you what, Kei?*" OldFish replied, pulling a soft mango toward their beak.

"About the other *Singer* DeepRunner led to the Koru-Kah!"

OldFish's eyes swiveled toward DeepRunner.

"Yes," Kei continued, "I see your sign clear enough under the waves. And my aunt told me. My aunt told me!" Kei paused, anger filling her voice as she asked, "How many others did DeepRunner take to the Koru-Kah? Where there more?"

"How many were lost, OldFish?" Her song ended, tones pulsing as her cheeks burned red.

OldFish's mantle turned blue, reply tinged with sadness and shame, *"I don't know, Kei."*

"But others went?" Kei asked.

"Yes, that's what I was told."

"And you were helping? You were going to feed me to the Koru-Kah?"

"No!" OldFish's mantle went colorless. *"No Kei. I would never do that."*

"So I am just your pet!" Kei sang, her melody crashing like storm waves on a long-forgotten beach.

"You are not! You are my friend. I came with you. To protect! I will not let the Koru-Kah take you. I came to help you, Kei! DeepRunner says the Koru-Kah leave their floating islands in family kayaks. We will speak to those. Not go near their islands. I will keep you safe!"

Kei's lips remained sealed. She glared at OldFish, then at DeepRunner.

"I am no one's pet," she said.

"You are not," OldFish agreed *"You are my friend."*

Gray silence covered DeepRunner, and his eyestalks retreated beneath the waves, avoiding Kei's gaze.

Kei's legs trembled in the water. Her fingers dug into the sand, and she sagged back onto the beach. Closing her eyes, a light breeze ruffled her lashes, the coolness a sharp contrast to the heat rising from her chest. Weight, like a clenched fist, squeezed her heart, pushing the breath from her lungs as her mind spun. Fragments of conversation swirled—DeepRunner, the lost Singers, her father's empty gaze. Her mother's steady hand, warm on her shoulder. And then the rush of water beneath her racing kayak, and trembling notes rising within her soul, spilling out into the world.

And then, that long-ago memory of OldFish's tentacles—strong, embracing her, pulling her to safety—flashed before her eyes. For a moment, nothing existed—except the memory of the storm, the thunder in her ears, and the ocean's power, dragging her under. She remembered breaking through the surface, gasping for air, gasping for life. But then the memory of OldFish faded, replaced by the sight of DeepRunner sinking beneath the waves.

From somewhere deep inside, her truest melodies welled up, carrying a strength that had long been contained within her heart, suppressed by fear of living. Her inner power erupted, her lips parting as her song poured out. Notes exploded from her throat, high and clear, striking DeepRunner's ear knobs with piercing clarity.

> *I swim the ocean sea*
> *And struggle over land*
> *I am Kei.*
> *My broken legs*

Have set me free
My song will save
Your children
I am Kei.
I will not bend to you!

Her voice fell silent. Here, endless miles from home, with only two kopri for company, a force stirred within her — a strength she had never known existed. She was Kei — not her legs — and she would face the world with pride!

Silence draped across the beach. OldFish moved away.

DeepRunner faded to gray, mango dropping from limp tentacles. The ancient kopri slipped into the water, sinking to the bottom of the tiny cove. There, DeepRunner's mantle flickered to a sandy brown, disappearing from the world.

Leaving Kei alone on the beach.

* * *

Before leaving the islet the next morning, Kei scraped the last shreds of clinging snail meat from the conch shell, then chipped the tip away against an outcropping of coral rock, allowing air to echo through its spirals. She placed the conch horn to her lips and blew a long note, which echoed over the mangroves and out over the open sea. The conch had a resonating bass tone, too beautiful to abandon on the beach. She wove a holder for the conch from thin twine and secured it to the prow of her kayak.

With that done, she pressed her hands into the sand and crawled back toward the tree line, dragging her legs behind her. She gathered the remaining fruits within reach and tossed them back into the water. Her fish-skin skirt hung in tatters, her thighs scraped and cut by sand, rock, and coral. She ignored the sting of salt in her wounds, focusing on the task at hand as she kept gathering food.

Sharing neither song nor kopri-sign, the three companions ate mangoes on the wet sand. The sweet, juicy flesh reminded Kei of breakfasts with her parents—her mother's smile as she peeled ripe mangoes, her father cracking nuts with one of his strike stones. But that was before the accident, when they had still lived together in the heart of their village.

But Kei's decisions had led her here. To this tiny islet with two kopri for companions. Sighing, Kei washed her hands in the surf and climbed aboard her kayak, pushing off and paddling away from the lonely beach.

The kopri gripped the kayak's tow ropes, and together, the three travelers surged across the rippling ocean. After half an hour of paddling through shallow waters, they reached a wide channel slicing into the Aguerda's tangled mangroves—a gateway to a strange and unfamiliar world. For a moment, she held her paddle still, gripped by hesitation, her thoughts drifting to the vast Menehko Ocean and the mysterious Koru-Kah. But there was no turning back. Her paddle plunged into the water, shivers running through its wooden handle. Kei leaned forward, driving the paddle deep and pulling hard, forcing herself to focus on the burn in her muscles rather than the dangers ahead.

The group's forward motion slowed as they battled a current flowing out of the channel. DeepRunner explained to Kei and OldFish that the currents switched direction twice a day, changing with the tides of Menehko, the outer sea. As predicted, at midday, the current changed, carrying Kei's kayak rapidly eastward toward the outer ocean — and the Koru-Kah!

According to DeepRunner, they wouldn't find more *deadwater* until after passing through the mangrove swamps, so Kei drank sparingly as they paddled deeper into the wilderness.

But food was abundant.

Periodically, OldFish lifted a wriggling catch from the water, gripping it tightly before slapping it onto the kayak. Kei took each offering, holding the slippery prey and carving off tender chunks with her flint knife, savoring the moist flavor as she chewed.

DeepRunner warned of the many dangers lurking in the mangroves and kept them near the center of the channel, where they spent their first night in the Aguerda swamp. Both kopri kept their tentacles wrapped around the kayak's tow ropes and sank to the shallow bottom, blending into their surroundings as they settled to sleep.

DeepRunner and OldFish took turns staying awake, keeping watch. Though the water had grown murky, their ear knobs quivered, attuned to every movement and danger around them. Kei could sleep without fear, OldFish assured her, as the current gently rocked her to sleep. If any predators had approached during the night, the kopri said nothing the following morning.

Kei's dreams were haunted by her mother's worried voice, her warnings sharpened by the staccato rhythm of her father's drums: *rat-a-tat-tat*. She awoke with dread clutching her heart, a nameless fear that lingered no matter how relentlessly she paddled.

Two more days dragged on, each one the same—paddling through the winding channel, as foreboding coiled tighter in her chest, unshakable and ever-present. At times, herons flew low above the water, hunting. Other times, the channel split, but DeepRunner always chose quickly, scenting the ever-present currents of Menehko, the great outer ocean.

As they neared the eastern edge of the brackish swamps, a wide, muddy bank rose from the channel's edge, where bright pink birds stood on stilt-like legs, their feathers striking against the murky, salt-tinged landscape. A hundred black eyes turned toward her, and when the kayak came too close, the flock of pink birds spread graceful wings and launched into the air. Flapping, spraying water. The pink birds skimmed west over the channel's water, turning a bend and disappearing, leaving Kei alone once more.

Kei glanced at the tow ropes and the thin piece of twine attached to both. If necessary, she could tug the twine to warn the kopri swimming below. Her gaze shifted east along the narrowing channel, scanning the muddy bank as she paddled. Further along, an old log lay half-submerged in the water, where the mangroves had closed in, leaving just a few kayak-lengths of open water. She noted its pebbled surface but thought nothing of the oddly shaped log.

Until it moved.

Until it languidly turned, pushing against the current.

Until Kei saw two yellow eyes open, staring from puffy hoods behind a long snout.

She grabbed the warning twine, yanking hard. The forward motion of the kayak slowed. The tow ropes sagged in the muddy water—with no sign of the kopri.

With rapid back thrusts of her paddle, Kei fled from the oncoming creature. But it approached faster than she could retreat. She saw a long tail, half the length of her kayak, swinging in undulating motions, driving the creature forward. As it neared, Kei could see a mouth below its long snout, lined with sharp teeth. Its yellow eyes, with black slits, tracked her every movement.

The kopri were gone, nowhere to be seen, and she could not escape the fast-approaching lizard. She recognized it from the stories told by hunters back home in Tirahanko Bay: a crocodile.

With a swift motion, she secured the paddle and pulled her fishing spear from its spot on the kayak's upturned bow. Her teeth clenched, lips turning white. Her heart pounded, sending spurts of hot blood through her veins. She raised the spear above her shoulder.

The crocodile opened its snout as it closed in. Rank on rank of fangs, like nothing she had seen before. Kei gripped the spear. Ready to defend herself. But her breath froze as dread settled in: she stood no chance against this ancient crocodilian monster.

Then, water churned as DeepRunner's gray tentacles shot up beneath the crocodile, wrapping around its body. Tooth-edged suckers on the tentacles latched onto the crocodile's hard scales and the soft leather of its underbelly. A shrieking hiss erupted from the beast as it flexed its tail. It rolled — faster and faster — a death roll meant to kill prey. But now, the crocodile fought only to shake DeepRunner loose.

As the crocodile rolled and spun in a savage frenzy, thrashing violently, DeepRunner's mantle whirled through the air. The two churned the water, sending up clouds of muddy white as they sank beneath the surface.

Then, a sudden silence, as the water turned to glass. Kei heard a bird calling, and the distant ripple of mangrove leaves. The yellowed underbelly of the crocodile burst to the surface, straining, heaving. DeepRunner's tentacles still engulfed the beast, slowly draining its strength, the once-deadly creature too tired to continue its death roll. For one long moment, the pair floated on the water's surface.

Then OldFish jetted from the deep, trailing a bleeding tentacle that dangled like a headless snake, held together only by strips of torn flesh. The kopri's smooth, jet-black skin glistened as they shot through the water, beak extended and mantle flaring wide. OldFish plunged onto the crocodile's belly, beak slicing downward, tentacles lashing around the beast. With each strike, OldFish's razor-sharp beak drove deep into the crocodile's soft underside, once, twice, thrice—each strike puncturing vital organs. Then, with a final thrash, all three combatants—crocodile, DeepRunner, and wounded OldFish— plunged beneath the water.

Silence descended as Kei's kayak steadied on the water— which turned red with crocodilian blood.

And then, she was alone.

Partners of the Hunt

"*ut it off,*" OldFish signed, thrusting a half-severed tentacle from the water. The mangled limb flopped onto Kei's kayak, splattering blue gore across the woven reed bundles. The sharp, coppery tang of kopri blood stung her nostrils — so different from the iron scent of the crocodile's red blood. Or her own. DeepRunner looked up from the crocodile carcass, subdued blue and black streaking their mantle.

"*Bite it off yourself. It grows back,*" the old kopri signed before ripping off another chunk of crocodile meat and pulping it with a tooth-lined tongue. Kei ignored DeepRunner, turning her attention to OldFish's pain.

"How much will this hurt?" Kei sang. She had seen injured kopri before, and knew their tentacles regenerated, but she had never helped care for a wound like this — let alone performed an amputation.

OldFish's skin pulsed feebly, signs dim as they said slowly, deliberately, *"I have separated my mind from the damaged tentacle. It can heal without me. Now cut it off."*

Kei grasped the still-healthy part of OldFish's mangled tentacle, pressing her knife against its undamaged flesh, saying, "But you won't feel it?"

"Make a clean cut," OldFish signed, ignoring her question, *"so the new tentacle grows faster."*

A slapping on the water caught Kei's attention. Before she could begin her cut, DeepRunner jetted to the far side of the kayak. The ancient kopri's mantle turned an unexpected brown, speckled with nurturing blue sympathy.

"Wait," DeepRunner signed, curling an appendage around OldFish's dangling tentacle, which writhed, solid red, squirming with pain. The limb flexed instinctively, its own rudimentary awareness reacting to DeepRunner's touch. As DeepRunner embraced the mangled appendage—still tethered to OldFish by scraps of living flesh—the severed portion faded from dark red to deepest gray, its struggling motions slowing, soothed by DeepRunner's gentle grip.

"Do it quick," DeepRunner signed, *"for both of them."*

Kei tightened her grip on OldFish, while DeepRunner steadied the dying limb. Her breath stilled. Then she sliced— fast and smooth—cutting cleanly through OldFish's soft tissues.

The amputated tentacle coiled in DeepRunner's grasp, still moving, still sensing. OldFish's stump flared a mottled red, pain streaking across their mantle in deepest burgundy.

Kei's stomach tightened, but she forced herself to breathe steadily, willing her nerves to settle. OldFish clenched their stump into a tight ball, staunching the flow, but blue gore had already splattered across Kei's kayak, slick and staining her hands.

Signless, OldFish curled inward, grey, and sinking slowly beneath the murky water, their movements sluggish and quiet. DeepRunner remained silent, gently caressing the severed tentacle, as if offering comfort to its fading awareness. The brain of a Kopri was spread throughout its body, each tentacle harboring its own rudimentary mind. Even now, the severed limb twitched faintly, a dim spark of life lingering, slowly fading beneath DeepRunner's tender touch.

DeepRunner cradled the dying tentacle, saying, *"Its awareness will hang on for hours, until it dies. I will comfort its passing."* Brown ridges rose and fell on DeepRunner's mantle, offering comfort and soothing sympathy to a dying creature.

Kei had once thought the surly kopri cruel or unfeeling, but as DeepRunner comforted the dying part of OldFish, she realized the haughty kopri reserved its hostility only for her — the human who DeepRunner reluctantly relied on. To its own kind, the ancient kopri showed tenderness and compassion.

Kei reached into the muddy channel, rinsing gore from her hands, then tossed handfuls of water onto her kayak, cleaning away the mess. But a stain from the kopri's copper-based blood remained on the reeds. Not bright red, like a human's, but dull teal, with hints of coppery-green.

DeepRunner sank into the murk, jetting slowly toward the bottom of the channel, the severed tentacle dangling from their beak. OldFish had contracted into a camouflaged lump on the bottom of the channel, but DeepRunner sensed the wounded kopri's presence. In the darkness, patterns of light pulsed on DeepRunner's mantle, like fireflies in rhythm—each glow shifting in sync with the silent language on their body, sending messages through the murky water.

"We can't stay here," DeepRunner signed. No answer came. *"There are more of them. The lizards. I know you want to hide and grow your tentacle. But not here. It is too dangerous."*

"How far?" A question formed on OldFish's skin, glowing dimly with phosphorescent light.

"We are almost through," DeepRunner replied. *"Before dark, we'll reach coral gardens beyond the swamp, where you can rest. Prey is easy to catch there, and I will feed you while you heal. But we must leave. I will tow the human's kayak, but you must swim. Now."*

Green spread across OldFish's mantle in agreement, tentacles uncurling—except for the stump, which remained tightly contracted as the wounded kopri rose to the surface. DeepRunner gripped both tow ropes with tentacle tips, their mantle swelling and contracting as they jetted forward, the dying tentacle trailing from their beak. Comforted by

DeepRunner's powerful presence, Kei paddled steadily, though her gaze still flicked warily to the mud-lined bank.

Hours later, the severed tentacle quivered once, then turned gray and hung motionless. DeepRunner's beak opened, allowing the dead tentacle to sink into the depths. OldFish swiveled one eye, tracking the lifeless appendage as it descended. The deepest blue of sadness rose in anguished puckering on OldFish's skin. Neither Kei nor DeepRunner could offer comfort. Instead, they pushed through the channel water with all their strength, seeking the safety of the outer sea.

By the time the sun had set behind them, the last of the mangrove swamps had thinned out and the travelers left the Aguerda. They had reached the edge of Menehko — the outer ocean — where a rainbow-hued coral garden stretched for miles in every direction. DeepRunner led OldFish to the center of the gardens, where the wounded kopri squeezed into a crevice at the base of a massive coral ridge. DeepRunner's mantle spread over OldFish's hiding place, camouflage rippling across their skin as both of the kopri melted into the reds, greens, and yellows of the living coral formations.

Not far off, the ridge widened and rose high enough for mangroves to take hold, their tangled roots floating above the water to form a small island in the heart of the underwater garden. Kei tied her kayak to one of the trees, then gripped the roots, hauling herself onto the sun-bleached coral. She left her canes secured to the kayak, dragging her stiff legs behind her. The islet was too small to offer a beach, and no mangoes grew here. Yet, she lay on the solid ground, safe from ocean predators, and fell into a dreamless sleep.

* * *

Two days they rested, there in the center of the coral garden, but Kei's fresh water supply was running low. According to DeepRunner, more *deadwater* could be found another day's travel southwest of the Aguerda. When the sun rose on the third morning, OldFish floated to the surface, greeting Kei with dim green and yellow crinkles around their eyes. Kei could see a shiny nub forming in the center of OldFish's truncated stump — a new tentacle growing out.

OldFish jetted in fits and starts, mantle gray in silence, as the group traveled above the vibrant underwater garden. Several times, DeepRunner whipped a tentacle into a crevice like a striking snake, pulling out a hapless crab and feeding OldFish. The brown sympathy painted across DeepRunner's mantle shocked Kei. Even more surprising was how DeepRunner refused to eat until OldFish's hunger had been sated. In that moment, Kei realized that the kopri she had known at home behaved the same — always looking out for each other. Lost limbs were a common injury for kopri, whose boneless tentacles and delicate skin made them vulnerable to the claws of crabs and the teeth of sharks.

But DeepRunner's compassion for OldFish did not extend to Kei. While Kei and OldFish served one another, like two halves of a clam shell working together, DeepRunner's mantle darkened whenever talking to her.

"How much longer," Kei sang to DeepRunner, when the surly kopri passed near her kayak.

"*Soon,*" DeepRunner replied, disdain painted in black circles around their eyes. "*I smell your deadwater.*"

"I see an island on the southern horizon. Is that it?" Kei asked. But DeepRunner made no reply, jetting away as their mantle faded to a silent gray.

Another two-hour paddle brought the group to the large island Kei had spotted, formed eons ago by a long-forgotten volcanic eruption. Following the scent of *deadwater*, DeepRunner guided Kei to a small stream-fed cove. Without a word, DeepRunner left her there, darting off toward a large reef that offered the recovering OldFish many places to hide.

Kei beached her kayak and untied her canes, pushing her stiff legs into the shallow surf and crab-walking onto dry sand. She dragged the kayak further up the shore, then hung empty waterskins around her neck before shuffling toward the small stream flowing into the cove.

Kei dropped to the ground at the stream's edge, greedily pulling handfuls of fresh water to her chapped lips. The cool liquid quenched the dryness in her mouth and throat, washing away an ever-present taste of brine. Thirst slaked, she plunged the waterskins into the stream. As the skins filled, the burbling of air mingled with the chirps of songbirds and the buzzing of insects, filling the cove with music.

After refilling her water containers, Kei began gathering *lobias,* tiny grapes that grew only near the sea. They hung in heavy clusters from the low branches of trees scattered along the edge of the cove. Each handful of the tiny purple fruit puckered her lips with tartness, but juice flowed over her tongue and trickled down her throat with each swallow — a welcome change from raw fish.

As daylight faded, the silence around Kei pressed heavily upon her, a weight that seemed to grow with each breath. But her friends were safe, and she had water, food, and solid ground beneath her.

Though no one was there to hear it, a song of gratitude began to form in Kei's mind — an old rhyme from her childhood, simple and familiar. It reminded her of her mother's arms, holding her close and singing her to sleep. Kei closed her eyes, letting the last rays of daylight warm her face, and in the stillness, she could almost hear her mother's song. It was a tender memory, woven with harmony and tone, accompanied by the soft rhythm of her father's drums.

Her father. Kei's chest rose as she breathed in, the thought pulling her deeper into the moment. He had loved her, despite his retreat into smoke. A smile spread across her sun-burned face. Her chest rose and fell with a quiet gratitude, for simply being alive, pouring out into the world.

The wind upon my back,
The Sun upon my face
Beneath my feet the earth
Holds my world in place

Thank you for the sunshine
Each new and rising day
And thank you for the love
You show in every way.

Thank you for the bounty
Of all the world around
And thank you for this moment
Of melody and sound.

At peace with her father, and lulled to sleep by the memory of her mother's arms around her, Kei sank into the warm sand. She tucked her arms beneath her head and drifted into a dreamless sleep.

* * *

Food and water were not a problem for Kei, but as the days passed by, restlessness set in. She spent much of her time paddling around the island, using her thin fishing spear to stalk prey. From time to time, she blew her conch shell horn, savoring its deep thrumming through the air. But the horn played only one note, too low for a kopri to hear, and offered little amusement. Though Kei found enough food to survive, she struggled to help feed OldFish, who stayed hidden while DeepRunner hunted for both of the kopri.

"*OldFish heals slowly,*" DeepRunner signed. The two of them, DeepRunner and Kei, bobbed on a calm stretch of water protected by coral columns. "*They need more food.*"

"I hunt all day," Kei replied. "There's just not much here." Prey fish near the cove were small—and well protected by the corals.

"*Yes.*" DeepRunner signed, mantle flushing green in agreement. "*I have not done better.*"

"We could hunt together." Kei said, keeping her voice high and steady, uncertain how the proud kopri would react to an offer of help. When DeepRunner kept their mantle gray, Kei sang on, "The corals here remind me of Tirahanko Bay. The ridges would block fish if we drove them into the reef. OldFish and I hunted like that at home."

DeepRunner did not reply, but an orange and turquoise questioning ridge rose around the ancient kopri's eyestalks—enough interest to encourage Kei to say more.

"At home," she said wistfully, "OldFish would camouflage in a bend of the reef, where the corals formed a pocket. I'd paddle out a little distance and wait for the fish to forget I was there. When prey passed beneath me, I'd slap the water with my paddle, driving them toward the pocket where OldFish was waiting."

"*I would not hunt?*" DeepRunner asked, orange and turquoise remaining bright.

"Not the way you usually do. But it would still be a hunt."

"*You would be the hunter?*"

"Yes, but you would make the kills," Kei replied.

A wave crashed further in toward the beach, echoing over the water while DeepRunner thought.

"*Where?*" the kopri finally asked. Kei pointed in reply. Nearby, coral columns formed a large, semi-circular ridge, creating an underwater bay on the ocean side of the reef. DeepRunner stared, unblinking, before flashing green and moving to a spot at the back of the bay, where they camouflaged themselves from view.

Kei stroked the water, moving her kayak east along the reef. Fifty Kayak lengths from DeepRunner's hiding spot, Kei turned, paddle held ready as she scanned for schools of prey fish. The tide crept up the beach before Kei's patience was rewarded. A school of silvery-blue *bigeyes* passed beneath her kayak, heading toward DeepRunner's hiding spot.

Using shallow strokes, Kei kept her kayak between the prey and the open sea. A hundred bigeyes gathered along the ridge, forming a shimmering wall of fat fish — each longer than her arm — their enormous, unblinking eyes bulged out, making them look larger than they were. Bigeyes! Just one could feed OldFish for days.

The bigeyes flitted along the submerged ridge. As the reef curved back to form an underwater bay, Kei began slapping the water with the flat of her paddle, chasing the school toward DeepRunner's hiding spot.

The multicolored corals exploded. What had appeared to be solid coral rock revealed itself to be DeepRunner, camouflage falling away as eight tentacles lashed out. Suckers slapped into the bigeyes' skin—hooking, digging, and dragging several hapless fish back to DeepRunner's waiting beak. The ancient kopri's mantle spread wide, forming a shroud larger than a kayak, before contracting to trap more bigeyes inside. With a swift, clean strike, DeepRunner's beak claimed its prey.

When Kei's kayak came near, DeepRunner's mantle shifted to light blue. Knobs rose in ridges of approval around their eyes. DeepRunner slapped a bigeye onto the reeds of Kei's kayak, bringing a smile to her face—perhaps, after all, they could be equals.

* * *

For Kei, the days passed in a blur. She and DeepRunner hunted daily, keeping OldFish fed while their tentacle regenerated. OldFish stayed huddled in a deep crack in the coral ridges, gray and silent. Healing.

"*OldFish is like a brooder, during spawn,*" DeepRunner signed one afternoon after a successful hunt. Another school of *bigeyes* had fallen prey to DeepRunner's camouflaged tentacles. After passing food to OldFish, DeepRunner and Kei floated together, savoring their own meals.

"A Brooder?" Kei sang.

"After the spawn," DeepRunner replied, ridges and knobs rising and falling in a slow but steady flow of signed words, *"The kopri who lays eggs. The one who stays in the nest until the hatch. That is the brooder."*

"Are you saying OldFish is a brooder? A woman?" Kei asked. Her voice rose high on the last word. Thinking about OldFish's gender shocked her. Kopri were just—kopri.

"I don't know." Yellow spirals smiled across DeepRunner's mantle, *"It is not their time."*

"How can you not know?"

"We are not like humans. For kopri, the change to brooder or guard happens only during spawn. After spawning we become just kopri again, neither brooder nor guard."

DeepRunner's mantle dropped to gray, and Kei chewed a slice of raw *bigeye*, thoughts racing with each bite.

"Which are you?" She asked.

A ripple of blue sadness swept over DeepRunner's scarred face.

"I stood guard twice when I was younger. The first time our younglings hatched, but there was so little food. We did not understand then. About the Koru-Kah and their nets. We watched our younglings grow. But there were so few fish, not even leafpeople floating on the surface for our younglings to eat. The Koru-Kah take everything. Our younglings starved. And the ones who survived,

their minds stayed dark. I watched for meaning in their camouflage. Tried to teach them speech. But our younglings remained stunted. Mute. Just wild octopus."

DeepRunner fell silent, even the scar beneath their eyes remained grey. When the old kopri said no more, Kei asked, "What about the second time? You said you stood guard twice."

DeepRunner's hooded eyestalks retracted into their mantle, lids closing as signs flickered just below the scar — which flared dark red.

"We tried again, SwimsAbove and I." Streaks of black and blue marred DeepRunner's signs as they spoke, sadness and resignation painted on their mantle. *"I couldn't protect her. Or our nest. Our eggs. The Koru-Kah came — with their nets."*

Splotches of bright crimson despair swept over the old kopri. *"I failed. Like I've failed all these years,"* DeepRunner's colors dimmed, grief pooling in slow, blue waves. *"Oh, SwimsAbove — the Koru-Kah are still out there. And now, my time is nearly gone. I'll be with you soon."*

Questions flooded Kei's mind: the spawning ground? Leafpeople? SwimsAbove? Kopri who could not sign, or think? She tried to make sense of what DeepRunner told her, but before Kei could ask questions, the ancient Prophet turned inky black and sank beneath the waves, hiding from the world.

On her kayak, Kei's breath caught, tears welling in sympathy for DeepRunner. Waves crashed over reefs. The call of a parrot echoed from the island's beach. Kei stared down at her rigid legs. Remembering her own grief. Remembering her father, lost in his pipe, smoking away his pain. She and DeepRunner shared more than she'd realized—both were marked by loss and the burden of events that could never be undone. But where Kei's grief—the accident that claimed her legs—was a wound that could never heal, the younglings of the Kopri still had a future. For them, she could sing for DeepRunner. For them, she could stand against the Koru-Kah.

For them, she would raise her voice, not in sorrow, but in defiance.

She shivered in the warm air, her eyes narrowing at the thought of the Koru-Kah's vast greed—and DeepRunner's eternal grief for his lost love, SwimsAbove.

"What will we sing to the Koru-Kah?" She asked DeepRunner, who had risen back to the surface. "What do you want me to tell them?"

For a time, DeepRunner's mantle remained dark blue, their tentacles still and limp. Then, the old kopri turned their gaze to the broken human who had become their friend. Kei was not Kopri—but she was a person.

Meeting her steady eyes, DeepRunner saw their mistake. Humans were not mere beasts, to be commanded. Lost in thought, signs flickered across the Prophet's skin. Always, DeepRunner had sought to control the humans, treating them as lesser beings. But now, grief wove into something new—a plea, not for power, but for peace. One equal to another.

And Kei listened, reading the grieving kopri's signs and shaping the sad story into a song for the two of them to sing together — to the Koru-Kah.

Woman from Beyond

After two weeks, OldFish's tentacle regenerated, allowing the three companions to renew their journey. Kei secured full waterskins and fresh fruit onto her kayak. With one last glance at the safety of the *deadwater* island, she pushed off, paddling into the uncharted waters of the Menehko Ocean. After two days of calm travel, storm clouds gathered on the horizon, and the wind rose in a furious howl. The waves reared up, sheer and towering, their crests curling overhead. Without the outrigger floats her father had installed, the storm's fury would have capsized Kei's kayak.

On that stormy day, the kopri pulled her up and over each billowing surge and she paddled madly down the other sides, laughing when the kayak hit the troughs between waves. And when the storm passed, Kei placed her conch shell horn against her lips, celebrating her survival with a long echoing blast. Then she slept, rocked to sleep by wavelets, with the coiling tentacles of both kopri woven protectively around her kayak.

The next day, DeepRunner said the kopri spawning grounds were near. By afternoon, the ocean floor rose beneath them. A forest of green seaweed fronds swayed, stretching a hundred feet from the sandy bottom. Great canyons split the emerald walls, where flickering schools of fish darted for cover. Coral columns jutted from the seagrass, sheltering crabs and eels, while barracuda prowled in the shadows.

The ocean grew shallower and shallower. The seaweed fronds gave way to white coral spindles, crystallizing near volcanic vents spewing hot mineral water into the sea. There, young corals bloomed—purple, red, and yellow—while swarms of tiny blue fish shimmered between ropy green fronds, basking in the warmth.

OldFish and DeepRunner blended into the brown reeds of the kayak, their skin shifting to match its hues. Below, the warm, clear water revealed a fairytale world—feathery white castles rising from rainbow-streaked reefs on the ocean's floor.

The tow ropes went slack. OldFish and DeepRunner floated to the surface, still camouflaged reed brown.

"We are here," DeepRunner signed.

"The spawning grounds," OldFish agreed.

Endless water stretched around Kei, unbroken to the horizon. But beneath the waves, crystal castles covered the ocean floor, sprawling as far as she could see.

Can you feel it?" OldFish signed. *"The current. The life rising from below?"*

"No," Kei replied. "Just water. Everywhere."

"The endless current of the outer sea flows here," OldFish signed, pink pebbles forming on yellowed skin. *"It warms the white gardens and cradles our unhatched eggs. After my mind awoke, my guard and brooder taught me the meanings of sign in this very place. But I have not felt this current since I left for the inner sea."*

The rainbow corals dazzled Kei, drawing her gaze to the seafloor, where translucent shrimp, krill, sardines, and tiny guppies swarmed, thriving in the mineral-rich waters gushing from heated cracks below.

"A feast for younglings," Kei sang, her voice catching in awe at the shimmering life below.

"It should be," DeepRunner flashed, black anger rippling through his signs. *"But what you see is only a drop of water compared to the bounty that once flowed here."*

"What do you mean?" Kei asked.

But DeepRunner faded to silent gray, lost in ancient memories, their tentacle coiling around a tow rope. OldFish took up the other rope while Kei paddled, and the spawning grounds drifted past beneath them.

As they moved further into the warm waters, Kei began to understand DeepRunner's words.

Throughout the center of the grounds, lines and trenches had been scraped through the crystal castles. Corals lay dead and broken on the seafloor, sea grasses torn from roots, littering the area with brown decay. And though fish still flickered through the wreckage, the bounty of the spawning grounds was diminished.

As the trio passed over a vast formation near the surface, mournful indigo rippled across DeepRunner's mantle. The ancient Prophet jetted to a crevice beneath them, followed by OldFish—whose mantle darkened, matching DeepRunner's deep blue grief.

There, amid shattered gray corals, an old kopri nest lay broken and exposed. Dozens of egg casings lay decaying among the scattered rocks and shells of the ruined nest. DeepRunner reached out, gently touching the broken eggs. But all that remained were dozens of partially formed beaks, too hard for even the tiniest of sea scavengers to eat.

Knobs and ripples of blue shimmered across both kopri as they entwined their tentacles, finding solace in each other's touch. DeepRunner's grief washed over them, a sorrow shared. Together, they mourned the ancient nest, crushed beneath the weighted ends of Koru-Kah trawling nets that had ground the seafloor into ruin.

Kei sat upright on her kayak, looking down through the crystal-clear water as her friends grieved.

A slow change began in the kopri. The ripples of their blue grief swelled, growing sharp and jagged. OldFish's mantle quivered, while DeepRunner's scar throbbed with crimson rage.

With a sudden jolt, DeepRunner jetted to the surface, pulling away from the wreckage of the nest, followed by OldFish. Their tentacles, no longer entwined in mourning, lashed out to take up the tow ropes. OldFish wept blue streaks, while DeepRunner's skin flamed with a desire for vengeance.

Kei's mind swirled with unspoken words—sorrow, sympathy—but nothing she could say would undo what had been lost. The grief of her friends echoed her own; no words had ever restored her legs.

She thought of the song she and DeepRunner had woven together—a plea for the lives of kopri younglings. How could the Koru-Kah not understand? Surely, once she explained, the masters of the floating islands would listen. Wouldn't they?

"We turn here. Swim against the current," DeepRunner signed, tugging the tow rope and angling south as they continued signing, *"The islands of the Koru-Kah drift with the current, dragging their nets behind them. They send great hunting kayaks ahead, searching for dolphin and tuna. If we move against the current, the Koru-Kah will find us."*

Kei nodded, then tapped her paddle twice against the water in agreement. With no further comment, the three companions turned south and pressed on against the current.

* * *

It appeared as a shadow on the southern horizon.

A splotch.

A speck.

Then, after the sun moved another hand's width in the sky, the speck became a black shape, separating from the horizon — small and formless — but its own thing, floating out there on the endless sea.

Kei stopped paddling and pulled the warning string attached to the tow ropes. Summoned, the two kopri floated to the surface. Together, Kei and the Kopri bobbed silently on the water, which had flattened beneath heavy, windless air.

"Something comes," Kei sang, her notes disappearing into the threatening emptiness around her.

"We see nothing below," DeepRunner signed.

"It is there," Kei sang, then fell silent.

For weeks, she had imagined this moment — rehearsing what she might say to the Koru-Kah, who lived on their floating islands. She had thought of how to plead with them, how to make them understand the harm they were causing.

Now, as the Koru-Kah loomed before her, all words fled.

She rubbed her right thigh, the muscle cramping worse than usual after days of lying motionless atop her kayak. "I can see it now," she sang, "A family kayak. Or something like it. I've never seen a boat so large."

"It is nothing." DeepRunner signed, *"nothing but a minnow compared to their floating islands."*

"It's coming toward us." Kei swallowed, her dry throat aching. She licked parched lips and reached for her half-full waterskin, tilting it to her mouth. The warm, leathery-tasting water coated her tongue, but she drank greedily. No need to ration it now — the time to sing had come.

But DeepRunner had lost other Singers to the Koru-Kah.

Kei hesitated, then set the waterskin aside, tying it back into place.

Time passed, and the black blotch on the horizon slowly transformed into a ship — one that would pass too far to the east!

Kei reached behind her seat, to the conch shell tied by a thin line to the kayak reeds. She filled her lungs, placing the horn to her lips, and blew a long throbbing note, echoing over the waves to the distant ship.

Which turned.

Changing direction and heading toward Kei.

As the Koru-Kah ship came into full view, OldFish and DeepRunner slipped beneath the waves. Kei felt the tow ropes go taut as she tightened her grip on the warning line that kept her connected to her friends.

The Koru-Kah ship approached. Longer than ten kayaks, the sides of the ship loomed out of the water and a single mast rose from its center, with a furled sail. Unlike the reed-bundled kayaks of Kei's people, the ship was built from dark, gleaming hardwood — a type Kei had never seen before.

Banks of oars extended from both sides, and crates and barrels were stacked neatly along its length.

Kei thrust her paddle into the water, driving her nimble reed kayak to the side of the ship, keeping a distance from it. Many strange-looking men, with glinting knives hanging from their hips, stood along the boat's railing, staring across the water at her. Fierce-looking men. With thick black hair gathered and bound in top knots, wearing cloth skirts, upper bodies bare and burnt dark by the sun. A man shouted a command, and the rowers lifted their oars, letting the ship glide to a halt.

Kei bobbed on wavelets, a stone's throw from the ship. A lump filled her throat, and her lungs felt heavy with salt air. She set her paddle lengthwise across the kayak and raised a hand, palm out. Licking her dry lips, she took a steadying breath and spoke.

"Greetings!" Kei said, pushing her melodious voice across the waves. "I am Kei. I must speak to you." The words of DeepRunner's message floated through her mind as she prepared herself to sing.

On board the ship, several men moved to face her, speaking to themselves. Then the largest of the men called back to her.

"Ei Ei, yamashii iti. V'Ahite!"

"I don't understand!" Kei shouted, letting the melody fade from her voice. She spoke slowly, hoping the Koru-Kah would comprehend. For now, her song was forgotten. "I must speak with you—about the kopri."

The large man laughed again, waving toward her as he spoke in a language unknown to Kei: *"Holo ika kopri. Varhneh tahn vaka. Ei, Ei!"*

Unlike the other men, he wore a leather band around his forehead, and a tattoo ran in black bands around his biceps.

In response to the man's words, twenty-four paddles lifted and stroked the water, spinning the Koru-Kah ship toward Kei. She yanked the signal string twice, then paddled hard, turning away from the oncoming Koru-Kah. The tow ropes snapped taut, and her kayak yanked around, heading away from the Koru-Kah boat, with the kopri jetting below.

"Holo maih V'Ahite! Yamashii!" The Koru-Kah man shouted. His harsh words had no melody and sounded like nonsense to Kei.

She paddled frantically away from the Koru-Kah, blood pounding in her ears as she gasped for air, straining to increase her distance from the wooden ship. Then a shudder struck the kayak, and she lurched forward. Motion stopped. The tow ropes remained tight, but a shiver raced through the kayak — which tilted beneath her, kept upright only by the outriggers on either side. Kei twisted around — and stared at an enormous fishing spear, large enough to kill a shark, piercing the kayak's stern.

The spear was attached to a rope, which pulled her kayak backward. Toward the Koru-Kah ship. Her paddle fought water uselessly. The sky wheeled above her, the world trembling in her eyes. Then the Koru-Kah ship slammed into the kayak's frail reeds, pushing its prow under the waves.

Diamond light cut her eyes as the sky rocked around her. The world heaved. Rough hands grasp her shoulders.

"Eheu!" a voice shouted from above, *"V'Ahite tahn ika!"*

Red pain shot through her shoulders as rough hands clawed into her skin, pulling her into the air. As she flailed helplessly, two tentacles surged from the sea, coiling around Kei's legs, trying to pull her free of the Koru-Kah. The razor-edged suckers bit into her ankles, drawing blood that dripped into the water. Then, a shadow streaked past her vision. A second spear struck deep into the tentacle's flesh. It uncoiled in pain, releasing her as the wounded kopri vanished beneath the waves.

Unhindered, the Koru-Kah sailors pulled her onto their boat.

Pain lanced through Kei's back. Red cuts and scratches blooming as the strange men dragged her over the splintered wood railing of the boat.

The last sight filling Kei's mind was blue blood, spurting from a severed tentacle slipping into the sea. And the last sound she heard froze her heart—the laughter of Koru-Kah men tossing her to the bottom of their boat, where her head struck wood and the world faded into nothing.

Alongside the Koru-Kah boat, the second spear floated in a pool of blue. But no sign remained of DeepRunner, whose severed tentacle tip writhed in pain as it sank beneath the waves. The harpooner retrieved his weapons and the large man, the captain, ordered the strangely built, lithe kayak tied off to the ship's stern. Then twenty-four oars slipped back into the water, the day's excitement over. And the Koru-Kah supply ship resumed its journey toward a freshwater harbor, still another day's hard rowing north.

The Number of her Tentacles

eepRunner swept their severed tentacle through the water, testing the damage where the harpoon had torn it away. With a slow contraction, they curled the tip into a puckered knob, staunching the blood flow and letting the wounded limb bear the pain alone. Only the very end had been sheared off; their movements beneath the waves would be slowed — but not stopped.

"*She is lost!*" Alarm streaked across OldFish's mantle.

"*We know where she is,*" DeepRunner replied.

OldFish whipped their tentacles in fury. "*The Koru-Kah have her! Like the others you brought.*"

DeepRunner stared at OldFish, purple rings pulsing around their commanding eyes as they signed, "*This is what **IT** came to do.*"

"*She!*" OldFish signed, flashing an angry red. "*Not IT. She is a person. She came to sing for you — not to be kora-kah prey!*"

The older kopri turned away, unable to face OldFish's anger. The purple rings around their eyes faded, as DeepRunner protested, *"She did what she came to do."*

But OldFish did not relent, *"we said she'd be safe!"* OldFish snapped. *"You said we'd pull her away if danger came."*

DeepRunner's colors drained, silent gray covering every tentacle — except the wounded one, which blazed red. Beneath their eyestalks, black and blue resignation pulsed in crisscrossing lines as they said, *"I did not know about their spears. Their ropes."*

"You didn't know?" OldFish's anger burned hotter. *"You swam all the currents of the world! How could you not know?"*

DeepRunner's signs stilled, then flickered again, defensive, *"I am no NetSinger. I can't see above the waves."*

"You fed her right to the Koru-Kah!"

"I did not." DeepRunner trembled. *"I did not know."*

All color drained from DeepRunner's mantle. The two kopri floated with the current, facing each other in silence. Then DeepRunner asked. *"Is one lost human too high a cost? Too great a price to save our younglings?"*

"DeepRunner!" OldFish shouted in purple ridges flaring around their eyes, flashing black again and again. *"Kei is a youngling too."*

"A human one. Why should that matter to me?"

Exasperated knobs puckered orange on OldFish's skin. *"She may mean nothing to you, but she swims in my heart."*

The orange puckering softened, fading into a smooth pink glow across OldFish's mantle. *"Does the number of her tentacles matter? Is that what makes us kopri?"*

"She is not kopri."

"Isn't she?" OldFish asked, *"Her thoughts reach me. Meaning swims in her song, no different from the thoughts painted on my mantle. What makes us kopri? The skin around our eye stalks? Or the mind and heart within?"*

DeepRunner signed no reply. Gray silence wrapped OldFish as well.

The two kopri drifted in currents, sensing the Koru-Kah ship rowing away. Heading north.

OldFish remained gray for a moment before turning from DeepRunner. With a sudden burst of speed, they jetted along with the current, chasing the stench of the Koru-Kah ship that fouled the waters of Menehko.

DeepRunner's purple mantle faded to gray, then they followed OldFish—no longer the commanding Prophet of the Deep—just an ancient, wounded kopri, whose choices had gone wrong.

* * *

Kei's eyelids fluttered. She lay in bilgewater, that smelled of urine and old sweat, with her forehead pressed against resin-soaked wood. In front of her, a forest of legs and bare feet stretched out. As she turned her head, the rowers came into focus. There were far more men than women, all burnished by the sun, their hands gripping long paddles affixed to the boat's railing by pivot latches. The rowers pulled in unison, their oars slicing through the water. Somewhere behind her, a drumbeat echoed, steady and relentless, keeping time with each stroke: *Bum-Boom, Bum-Boom, Bum-Boom.*

A thin trickle of blood had dried across her forehead, leaving a crusted line on her skin. Kei cracked her eyes open, letting only a sliver of light slip through her thick lashes. Trying to think. How long had she been unconscious? Where were her friends?

"Ar-Kora!" A harsh staccato voice called, floating somewhere above her.

Hard fingers jammed into the corded muscles of her legs. Poking, prodding, feeling her weakness. A man's calloused palm skimmed over her thigh as he muttered words Kei couldn't understand: *"Kaikia! Iā me varhneh."*

Kei held back a shiver, her lungs aching, her body frozen in the stinking water, as the poking, prodding fingers assessed her arms and shoulders. The rough hands brought goosebumps to her bare skin where they touched her, probing, as if she were a large tuna being prepared for slaughter.

"E holo varhneh. Kōkua lumi!" The strange words battered her throbbing head, their meaning lost on her.

Laughter rang out above her—not from the rowers, who pulled their oars to the steady rhythm of the drum, but from a group of Koru-Kah men beyond her sight, hidden behind crates and barrels.

The man standing over her stepped back, his feet splashing through the stagnant, foul-smelling water. A stench of fish rot and human sweat clung to the air, thick enough to taste. As the sun beat down on her again, Kei squeezed her eyes shut, willing herself to stay still. Thoughts tumbled through her mind — jumbled images, raw emotion. She tried to focus, but couldn't. No melody formed, and she ached to feel the familiar tentacles of OldFish gently embracing her.

The Koru-Kah had speech, but their words gnawed at her mind, sharp and discordant, battering her ears like the hollow clatter of crab claws scraping against stone. Kei curled her fingers into a tight fist, pressing against the nausea roiling in her stomach. The drumbeat pounded through her skull — Boom. Boom. Boom — each thump echoing with relentless force. Not the joyous rhythms of her father's drums, but a lifeless thrum that rattled through her clenched teeth.

Then, a new voice — gentle and lilting — whispered in her ear. A young man sat on a short bench behind her, his strange melody floating softly through the heavy air: "Shet schtill, gurl. Rezt vhile thee kahnst."

A suffocating fog clouded her mind as she struggled to grasp his meaning, though his hushed tone was unmistakably clear: *rest while you can.*

She exhaled, letting her eyes slip shut. The ship rocked, sending bilgewater sloshing over her, its rancid stench curling in her nose. An aching dizziness spread from the gash on her scalp, spinning the world around her and twisting her stomach into a sick knot. The drumbeat pounded on—Boom, Boom, Boom—steady and indifferent. Darkness crept in, swallowing her once more.

* * *

Kei awoke to the young rower's hushed voice pulling her from a painful sleep.

"Gurl, vee art in the harber. Thee muscht git up." He tapped her shoulder gently. "Git up, or dey vill trow thee o'er the side."

Kei groaned, her head and body aching, thirst rasping at her throat. Still, she pushed herself upright, leaning against the boat's smooth wood side. The sun had climbed to its late-morning position—she must have lost an entire day recovering from the blow to her head. The reed sail hung furled on the mast, and the ship lay still—they were no longer on the open sea.

"Vee art in the harber. I musht help unlood the boot. Here, drinke," the rower said, his oddly accented voice steady as he handed her a leather waterskin. She gulped down the tepid water, then turned toward the rower. He looked much like any young man from her own island, except for his uncut hair, which flowed past his shoulders in a thick black mane, bound with twisted reeds.

The water left a leathery bitterness in her mouth, but moistened her parched tongue and lips enough that she could speak.

"Thank you," Kei said. The young man only nodded, offering a small smile and a shrug. She realized he was not much older than herself. Her breath caught as she noticed a series of angry scars lacing his back. Then her gaze fell to his left cheek—a burn had left a distinct pattern on his skin. Not a random scar, but an intentional mark, raised and deliberate. Just like the maker's mark her father carved into his drums.

A brand.

The young man patted the bench in front of her and pointed at the oar. "Git up, gurl. Thee musht row ven we leave Ar-Kora harber." His words carried an odd melody, but their meaning was clear. She had to be ready to row when they left the harbor—named Ar-Kora, if she had understood correctly.

Her temples throbbed, and the world tilted around her as she pushed herself upright on the bench. She sat near the stern—the rear of the boat—with her back to the bow, the ship's front. Glancing over her shoulder, she took in the stacked crates and barrels lining the deck. Above her, the single mast loomed, its sail furled.

The young man locked his eyes on hers. "Goode. Vhen we leave Ar-Kora, thee musht row if thee want to live," he said, his voice gentle and sounding more familiar each time she heard him speak. Then he turned, hoisted an empty water barrel onto his shoulders and walked away.

Kei stared at the young man's scarred back as he joined a group of branded rowers carrying empty water casks along a wooden dock. Tearing her eyes from his scars, she took in the Koru-Kah themselves—taller than the men from her island, with wide, narrow eyes and crooked, hawk-like noses. Their straight hair was cut short, with oiled black strands plastered against their skulls in a bowl-like shape, covering their scalps from ear to ear and down to the nape of their necks. On top, thick bristles of longer hair were gathered into tight knobs, bound with leather thongs.

From her place on the rower's bench, she caught the gleam of light on long, sharp blades strapped to Koru-Kah waists— crafted from a shiny material unlike anything Kei had seen before. The Koru-Kah moved among the rowers, shouting orders in their unintelligible language, and occasionally striking a rower with a long wood cudgel. Some of the rowers looked like her guards, with the same midnight hair, sharp noses and narrowed ebony eyes. One rower had skin lighter than she had ever seen. Nearly the color of white sand, with yellowish hair. But most of the rowers appeared like people from her own tribe: brown sun-burnished skin, flowing black hair and wide amber eyes.

Disturbingly, she noted that every rower bore a brand seared into their cheeks—each marked with a different design. Scars crisscrossed most of their sun-darkened backs, mirroring those of the young man who had helped her. Bruises laced their arms and legs, the remnants of punishing cudgel blows.

The Koru-Kah leader stood alone on the dock. His hair was uncut, a leather headband gathering a black mane at the top of his head, where it arched backward before cascading down his spine. Beneath his eyes, dark tattoos etched his skin, while jagged black bands snaked around his upper arms. The leader ignored her, calmly counting piles of bananas and root vegetables.

Several other boats were tied to the dock, including two sleek ships with banks of oars on either side. They were built from the same dense wooden planks as the cargo ship beneath her. Having known only the mangroves and palm trees of Tirahanko Bay, Kei had never seen wood like this — thick, solid, and heavy. She had never even imagined trees so massive could exist, let alone that entire ships could be built from them.

Her gaze traced the length of the sleek vessels, and realization struck — they were war canoes, built for speed. She shook her head in disbelief. War canoes! Like something from a legend come to life. Nothing like them existed in the peaceful islands of the Nadako Sea.

Ar-Kora harbor sprawled beneath the jungle-clad slopes of a towering mountain. A wooden palisade encircled the bustling Koru-Kah village, wedged between the mountain and the docks. At its center, an enormous gate stood open, granting passage through the fortifications that guarded the settlement.

From her vantage point, Kei watched as rowers from the supply boat hauled empty casks up a stone-paved avenue leading into the village. The road wound between dozens of longhouses before vanishing behind the palisade walls. Moments later, other rowers emerged from the gate, staggering under the weight of full casks of water.

Standing high on the Palisade stood more Koru-Kah guards, holding spears and staring with dull, bored eyes at the workers struggling beneath their burdens. Above everything, on a high escarpment looming over the town, teams of workers bustled, raising more wooden walls and platforms. They were building a fortress to protect Ar-Kora's harbor entrance, though from what enemy, Kei didn't know. Nor could she guess. The scene before her was beyond her imagination.

The Koru-Kah leader glanced toward Kei, narrowing his eyes and twisting his lips in a hard frown. Kei quickly pulled her legs into a rowing position, with her feet thrust under a brace beneath the bench in front of her. Her inflexible legs, thus secured, would hold her in place, allowing her to pull an oar with force. She reached out and lifted the oar, held firmly in its pivot beside her rowing bench. She pulled the oar toward her chest, testing its weight and balance. The Koru-Kah leader kept blank eyes on her for a moment, then returned to his work.

For a time, she sat alone on the boat, hunched over her oar. The rowers and guards went ashore, gathering food, water and cargo, leaving her unbound. She thought about escape, but where could she go? Her kayak had been tied to the back of the boat; the Koru-Kah seemed intrigued by its reed construction, so different than their heavy plank-built ships. But even if she managed to reach the kayak, the guards patrolling the palisade walls would see her before she could paddle away. As for escaping through the village and into the jungle? Impossible. Too many guards. Too many spears. And her canes were missing. Kei had no hope other than to remain where she sat.

And so, the Koru-Kah left her alone. She was too useless to bother with. Her head throbbed. She thought of her mother — of songs rising over the warm waters of Tirahanko Bay. Her stomach rumbled with the memory of fish stew, simmering in pots on the black crystal sand of the bay. Tears blurred her vision, but she was too parched to cry. She had left everyone and everything she loved behind.

For this.

For a foreign harbor, the weight of wooden cudgels, and the voices of the Koru-Kah, their words as strange and unyielding as the ships that carried them.

The sun climbed another hand's width in the sky, and the boat was nearly loaded when Kei felt the oar shift in her grip. She frowned, tracing the oars length with her eyes. At the water's surface, where the paddle met the waves, a tentacle — its tip camouflaged in the same brown texture as the wood — had curled around the oar.

A quick glance to the dock, at the Koru-Kah with their shining blades, assured Kei that no one else had spotted OldFish lurking in the water.

Kopri signs rippled urgently just below the surface, *"Jump, Kei. We will swim you to safety."*

Kei nodded, acknowledging her friend. A trembling ran through her arms as she tensed, preparing to slip over the side and escape.

"*Hurry,*" OldFish signed. But Kei paused. The young rower — the one who had shown her kindness — returned to the boat. He called out to one of the guards, in the Koru-Kah language, seeking permission before stepping back onto the boat with a full water cask resting on his scarred back. The sound of the young man's voice lingered in Kei's mind, its cadence a blend of her own language and the sharp, staccato tones of the Koru-Kah. His words wove together like two entwined melodies. Her breath caught, heart pounding. A realization struck her — through him, she could learn to sing DeepRunner's song to the Koru-Kah!

Alone on the boat, Kei moistened brine-dried lips and began to sing, barely loud enough for OldFish to hear. She turned her face to the sky, as if she were singing to herself.

"I can't," she sang, "I must learn to sing to them. In their own words."

A white ridge rose around OldFish's ear knob, "*No!*"

"Stay near, OldFish, stay near," Kei sang. And then she cut off her song, as the young man and a Koru-Kah guard approached. OldFish released the oar, and when Kei glanced back toward the water — her friend was gone.

* * *

When the last water casks and crates of fresh fruit were lashed to the deck in stacks as high as a tall man's head, the drum began to beat, *bum-boom, bum-boom,* and the Koru-Kah Captain, called Ki-Kuna by his men, shouted his orders.

"Nui hiki!" came Ki-Kuna's harsh voice, lacking melody in Kei's ears. Kei mirrored the actions of the other rowers, who pulled their oars in a backstroke, reversing the boat away from the dock. Twelve rowers to a side, but not all were the same men and women who had arrived at the harbor. Kei had taken the place of one, while several others had remained in Ar-Kora, replaced by fresh laborers. Yet the young man who had given her water still sat on his same bench near her, smiling as she pulled her oar in a steady stroke.

Her lips twitched in a silent reply, but she tightened her grip, her knuckles white. Her gaze flitted from one rower to the next, taking in the unfamiliar faces. Finally, she turned to the young man, her eyes questioning.

He whispered a response, but his words only puzzled her — something about too many rowers speaking the same language. Why would their captors care about that? Before she could ask, a guard shouted, cutting off the conversation and forcing her to swallow her questions.

Kei kept her expression blank, lips pressed together. Her ears throbbed, but she forced herself to match the rhythm of the other rowers, gripping her oar and pulling again and again. She let the ragged sound of her breath mask the trembling in her heart.

"Goode. Dat is goode," the young man whispered, as Kei flexed muscles grown strong from many years of kayaking.

"_Ka hemah, heilah!_" Captain Ki-Kuna yelled when the boat reached the center of Ar-Kora's harbor. The rowers on Kei's side of the boat raised their oars from the water, while the rowers on her left continued paddling. The ship pivoted toward the mouth of the harbor. Four rowers sprang to their feet, hoisting the lone sail up the mast. As the wind filled the canvas, the vessel surged forward, gliding beneath the escarpment and the partially built fortress rising above its slopes.

"_Nua Oloula!_" Ki-Kuna ordered, and twenty-four oars dropped into the water. Kei copied the actions of the other rowers as the supply boat sped toward the open sea, leaving Ar-Kora's harbor and fortified village behind.

By the time the sun moved three hands in the sky, rowing had become routine for Kei. She was suited to the effort, finding it little different from paddling a kayak laden with fruit. While rowing, the young man beside her kept up a quiet stream of words. At first Kei paid little attention, focusing on gaining a rhythm to her rowing, but during a short rest break, he called to her insistently, tapping his fingers to his chest and saying, "Yakutee," repeatedly.

Kei turned her head, eyes blank as she watched the young man continue tapping his chest.

"Yakutee," he said.

Her lips curved up as part of his song came into tune. "Kei," she replied, tapping her own chest. In response, the young man grinned and pointed at her.

"Kei. Thy nahm ist Kei," he said. She grinned, then pointed back at him.

"Jacuti." She said, using her own Nadako accent. "Your name is Jacuti."

Before they could say more, the drumbeat began again, and they resumed rowing. But Jacuti kept talking.

"Oore," he said, tapping his oar with the palm of his hand.

"Oar," Kei repeated, tapping her own oar in reply.

A broad smile crossed Jacuti's sun-bronzed face — then faded as his eyes fell on Kei's legs.

"Thy leghes," he said, tapping his own leg.

Kei frowned, glancing down at her legs, which extended stiffly beneath the support beam of the bench in front of her.

"My legs?" she asked, tapping her thigh, her eyes narrowing.

"Yah, thy leggs," Jacuti repeated, tapping his leg again. "Kanst thou valk?"

Throughout the morning, Kei had come to understand the melodies of Jacuti's speech. His words reminded her of two harmonies, sung with a syncopated rhythm that merged into one new, unfamiliar chord. More and more, she could hear his meaning behind the notes of his accent.

"My legs," Kei murmured, a sigh escaping between pulls of her oar. "No. I cannot *valk* — walk."

"How longe til thee kanst valk? Art thee gitting bedder?"

"I won't get better," she replied. "I can't walk without my canes."

"Thy cahnz?"

"Yes. My canes. *Cahnz.* Sticks that hold me up when I walk."

"Thee needest — canes — to valk?"

"Yes. I need canes to *walk.*"

Jacuti stared at Kei's stiff, unbending legs, jammed beneath the forward bench as she rowed. He pulled his oar ten times, silent in thought. On the tenth stroke, he turned his head.

"Thare —" he said, glancing toward the back of the supply ship, where her kayak bobbed, tethered to the Koru-Kah vessel. "Be dey thy — *canes?*"

Kei followed his gaze. When she saw her canes tied to her kayak, relief crashed over her so completely that all she could do was nod.

Jacuti's eyes narrowed. When he spoke, he turned his head — not looking at her legs, but at her arms and hands, pulling strong and steady on the oar.

"Vell, thee art strong." His words hung in the air between them. "Vhen we get to the *Apum-ka*, mine muhter kanst help thee."

"Muhter?" Kei replied. She started to ask a question, but suddenly a shout rang from the front of the ship.

The drumbeat stopped, and the captain yelled, "*Aulöla pau!*"

Twenty-four oars withdrew from the water, and the ship slowed to a stop. Rowers exchanged furtive glances beyond

Jacuti's side of the boat. Water casks and fruit crates blocked Kei's view, but Jacuti whispered to her as he peered over the railing.

"The harpooner. He sees somethin'." Jacuti pointed to a spot twenty yards from the ship, his eyes alight with excitement, "a Kopri!"

Kei's breath caught as she followed his finger to a dark mass floating just beneath the water—where an eyestalk pushed up above the waves.

DeepRunner!

There was nothing Kei could do. Before she took her next breath, the unseen harpooner threw his barbed spear, but DeepRunner plunged beneath the waves, vanishing in a swirl of foam. As the harpoon flew across the water, the oar lurched in Kei's hand. She whipped her head around, eyes stabbing toward the tip of her oar—where OldFish gripped the wood, flashing urgently.

"Jump, Kei. Jump. Their floating island is near."

A shout behind her grabbed Kei's attention. She turned and spotted the harpoon floating on the waves. The harpooner had missed. DeepRunner thrust an eyestalk above the water again—taunting—and the harpooner took the bait, releasing a second harpoon.

All eyes but Kei's tracked the second harpoon in flight. She turned her gaze back to OldFish, singing quickly, with a high breathy voice.

"No. They hear me, OldFish. I will speak with them."

"If you go to their island. You will never return."

Her heart stopped. Breath freezing in her lungs. Kei remembered her aunt's warning of the Singers already lost to the Koru-Kah. She wanted to jump overboard and let OldFish tow her to safety, far from the violent Koru-Kah. But an image of the shattered spawning ground stood between her and the freedom of the sea. How could she abandon the Kopri?

Kei shook her head, drew a steady breath, and sang to OldFish: "I can jump later. From the island. Keep watch for me."

"Please Kei," OldFish signed, mantle turning a fearful black.

"Watch for me," Kei sang, "Now go."

OldFish floated motionless for a moment, then released the oar and sank back into the sea. Kei turned, looking for DeepRunner, but the ancient kopri was nowhere to be seen. Both harpoons floated unbloodied on the waves, attached to the ship by thin tethers.

The captain cursed, *"Yamahuni!"*

Ki-Kuna's angry voice stormed across the waves. He struck the nearest rower with his hard wood baton, venting his anger. *"Yamahuni kopri!"*

The harpooner drew his spears back onto the ship, and the drumbeat began again. The boat lurched forward. Kei glanced at Jacuti as they pulled their oars in unison. He met her gaze, his expression shifting—questioning, wondering—before his eyes drifted past her, fixing on the tip of her oar, where OldFish had been.

"Thee talkt to the Kopri. Thee sang to it!" He shook his head, eyes flying wide, "Thee art a **Singer**! Like mine muhter!"

Before Kei could reply, Captain Ki-Kuna took several quick steps toward Jacuti, his wooden club swinging with a sharp crack against the young man's shoulders, demanding silence. The blow knocked the breath from Jacuti, and a new bruise began swelling under the scars on his back.

But he grinned anyway, continuing to smile at Kei as he rowed.

The Floating Island

For a full day and night, the ship pressed east, rowers working in shifts through the endless darkness to keep the vessel moving. By the time the scorching midday sun rose on the second day, Kei's shoulders were taut with tension. No wind stirred the sail, and pure human sweat drove the ship forward.

"Tomay teho!" the Koru-Kah captain shouted, ordering the oars banked. Kei sagged forward, her muscles burning. Her head hung, chin pressing to her chest as she drew in ragged breaths, willing the relentless throbbing in her arms and shoulders to stop. She licked her dry, cracked lips, but the guards remained still, making no move to pass around the waterskins.

A quick glance toward Jacuti was no comfort. He too sagged forward, twisting his neck side to side to loosen knotted muscles. He managed a brief nod in her direction, nostrils flaring at the sting of salted air.

Captain Ki-Kuna barked another order, and two scarred rowers sprang to the anchor, dropping it into water grown shallow. A jolt shook the ship's wooden planks as its forward motion lurched to a stop. It shuddered, then rocked gently in the endless currents of the Menehko Ocean.

Only then did the guards pass out the waterskins, and when it was her turn, Kei gulped warm water tinged with the taste of aged leather, as if it were fresh from a cool mountain spring. After passing the waterskin to Jacuti, Kei noticed that the few women among the rowers had thickly muscled shoulders and arms — hardened and strong, like hers, from years of rowing.

As she watched, another rower — barely more than a boy — leapt to obey an order from the Captain, scampering up the towering mast. Kei held her breath, expecting him to fall at any moment. The mast swayed with the ocean swells, but the boy moved with it, his body rocking in rhythm as he climbed, hands gripping the belaying pins driven into the mast to form a sparse ladder. Soon, the boy stood atop a small platform, arms wrapped around the tip of the mast, as he began scanning the far horizon.

The tip of the mast pitched wildly with each swell, arcing high above the waves. Breath caught in Kei's still-heaving chest as she watched the boy reach the end of each swing, momentarily suspended over the open sea.

"*Mascht Apum-Ka,*" the captain yelled to the boy, who nodded and kept his gaze on the waves. Ki-Kuna grinned as he watched the boy, and called out a rough joke to his men:

"*T'mimusu! Māhk oma!*"

The Koru-Kah guards roared with laughter, but Kei understood none of their words, nor why they laughed. Their tuneless speech held no meaning, no more intelligible than the raucous call of seabirds.

Yet Jacuti's voice — his song — was different. More and more, its melody wove into her own. He translated for her when needed, but this time, he only shrugged, frowning.

"What did he say?" Kei asked.

Jacuti slid his eyes away from her face. "Nuthin'. Nothing. A stoopid joke." His gaze tightened into thin slits as he tracked the boy swinging above the sea. "Kan't thee understand them?"

"No. And sometimes, I have trouble understanding you, too."

Jacuti's lips curved into a small smile. "Thee speaketh like my muhter. She will be glad to talk vit thee."

Then a guard yelled, stopping their conversation with a club smacking Jacuti's back — hard enough to bruise skin, but not damage the muscles needed to pull his oar.

After that, the boat rocked for hours on four-foot swells, with no land in sight. The rowers slumped in their seats, sleeping, or just staring out to sea. When the waterskin passed to Kei again, she drank greedily, warm water moistening cracked lips. The guards passed out tiny, dried fish, which crunched when Kei bit into them. She ate without thinking, her body famished by so many hours of labor.

Finally, a cry rang out from above. The boy shouted from atop the mast, his arm stabbing toward the southwest. *"Apum-ka!"* he yelled, his voice sharp with excitement.

"Tomay tohchrah!" Captain Ki-Kuna barked, ordering the boy to back the deck, and the anchor to be raised.

The boy spidered down the swaying mast. By the time he reached his seat, the anchor was stowed and twenty-four oars had dropped into the water. The supply boat lurched forward, turning in the direction the boy had indicated.

The drumbeat quickened, and Captain Ki-Kuna stalked among the rowers, brandishing his wooden cudgel, barking for more speed. Kei hauled on her oar, her hands jolted by each slap of the blade against the water. She leaned back, fingers tightening, shoulders and biceps flexing with every pull. Her shoulder blades clenched together, muscles taut with a fiery ache. Urgency gripped the ship as guards and rowers alike strained to reach their destination. The drums pounded double-time—*boomboom, boomboom, boomboom*—driving each stroke, rattling through her skull.

Strangely, a song lyric composed itself in Kei's mind as she rowed, the words echoing in time to the memory of her father's beating drums.

Bum-boom, Bum-boom
The drums at noon

Pounding over our head
Bum-boom, Bum-Boom
The drums resume
Keep time until you're dead.

The lyrics were nonsense, but the pounding drum sank deep into her, awakening the rhythms her father had gifted her. She couldn't stop the lyrics from repeating in her mind. With each pull of her oar, the refrain echoed — *bum-boom. bum-boom* — over and over, as the exhausted rowers held to the quickened pace.

The sail remained reefed, useless as the boat drove into the wind, its prow cleaving through rolling swells. Cresting waves slammed into the hull, spraying Kei's back with salty brine that stung as it dried in the brisk sea breeze. Above, a clear blue sky stretched unbroken from horizon to horizon. Yet Kei's world shrank, containing only her oar and the relentless drumbeat pounding in her ears.

Bum-boom. Bum-boom. But then Jacuti's voice called out, interrupting the relentless drumbeat.

"The *Apum-Ka*," He said, twisting his chin toward the prow of the boat. "Vee'll be home soon."

Between strokes, Kei turned her head. A tiny black dot on the horizon swelled, growing larger with each passing moment. Her knuckles whitened on the oar, muscles taut with strain. She gulped quick breaths, her mouth opening and closing, words forming but swallowed before they could escape. Almost, she asked Jacuti a question — almost — but fear of the Koru-Kah cudgels kept her silent. So she rowed, withdrawing into herself, saying nothing.

DeepRunner's words in Tirahanko Bay weeks ago echoed in Kei's mind: *"These invaders sing no words. They read no signs. Like beasts, their skin is mute."*

In the safety of Tirahanko Bay, the journey had seemed so easy. An adventure, traveling with the kopri, escaping her father's hut and her mother's constant demands.

Kei glanced at Captain Ki-Kuna as he struck a rower — for no reason she could see, other than cruelty. Moisture gathered in the corners of her eyes, but she blinked hard, refusing to cry. Even if the Koru-Kah could understand the song she and DeepRunner had written, could such bestial people care about the fate of her kopri friends?

Ki-Kuna maneuvered the ship into position north of the Apum-Ka, then ordered the crew to hold steady. Kei twisted her head, eyes locked on the approaching colossus as it drifted toward them on the current.

It loomed larger than Tirahanko Bay. Larger than her entire village. Larger than the islands where she and the kopri had rested during their journey.

So — this was the "floating island" the kopri had spoken of.

The Apum-Ka reminded her of Mount Jikea, its sloping sides rising steeply before descending into a vast, bowl-shaped crater. The vessel's curved outer edge rose three kayak lengths above the sea, its hull like a hilltop ridge, enclosing a hidden interior. Built to flex with the waves, the Apum-Ka moved with the ocean's swells rather than resisting them.

From within its protective hull, a towering wooden structure jutted skyward — a forecastle immune to the wind that whipped white spume against the sloping sides. At its peak, an observation deck overlooked the endless sea, and from there, a slim mast reached a dozen kayak lengths into the sky, swaying with the breeze.

Kei's gaze traveled up the length of the mast, to a small platform where two figures, barely visible, scanned the ocean surrounding the Apum-ka. Several Koru-Kah stood on the rooftop observation deck, yelling orders to different parts of the vessel.

Kei bit down on her lower lip, chewing it nervously. Her breath quickened into shallow pants, heat blooming across her face as her heart raced. How could she ever face the Koru-Kah on that command deck, let alone speak to them? And without her canes, how could she even cross the gangway and climb that towering hull?

Kei's gaze followed a seagull, soaring effortlessly across the vast expanse of the Apum-Ka. Vertigo struck her as she watched the floating island ride the swells, molding itself to the shape of waves rippling beneath it. The Apum-ka sprawled across the ocean, so large its own flock of seagulls called it home.

"*Hemah tehoss!*" Captain Ki-Kuna yelled. By now, Kei had come to understand his guttural words: "Raise Oars."

After retracting their oars, the rowers sprang to their feet, gripping the ropes and hauling the supply ship toward the Apum-Ka. Dock workers, each marked with a brand of ownership burned into their cheeks, tied the supply boat to the massive vessel.

Nearby, another supply ship and several smaller fishing boats—harpoons jutting upright from their bows—were moored against the Apum-Ka's dock. Among them sat a sleek craft, its long, tapered bow and stern built for speed. Fifteen oars lined each side, leaving little room for cargo. A warship, Kei thought with a chill.

All the ships were built of the same dense wood that Kei had never seen before, a material unlike anything she had encountered. Even the smaller rowboats, unlike her own kayak made of bundled reeds, were crafted from solid wood. She glanced at the rowboats, wondering if they would flounder in the surf, rather than skip across the waves like her own lithe kayak.

Beyond the boats, the sides of the Apum-ka curved out of sight, whitecaps crashing from time to time against the sloping hull.

Movement swirled around Kei, workers rushing to and fro as wooden gangplanks thudded onto the railing of the supply boat. Beyond the narrow dock, the Apum-Ka's hull loomed, rising sharply like a steep hill from the ocean. A sudden shock rippled through her— neither the dock nor the hull was made of wood, like the ships, but instead from bundled reeds, similar to those in her own kayak. The Apum-Ka was constructed of massive reed tubes, stacked layer upon layer, running in endless lengths around its circular hull. Along the raft's edge, wooden shafts as thick as her arms jutted outward at odd angles, their purpose unclear.

Ropes tied the curving reed bundles tightly together, creating an unexpectedly firm surface. Wooden planks stretched across the reed surface of the dock, leading to a gangway as wide as her kayak. Workers carried crates and water casks up that wooden path, disappearing over the hull's top into the unseen interior of the Apum-Ka. Like the rowers on the boat, the workers came from different tribes, some stocky and short, some tall and lean. A wild mix of strangely colored hair, some thin and straight, others a mass of curls. But the Koru-Kah were everywhere—moving among the branded workers, cudgels raised and blades glinting menacingly.

Kei looked back over the ocean and imagined the eyes of a kopri poking out of the water. She swallowed, a sour taste in her mouth, then turned again to the docks of the Apum-Ka. Workers began carrying crates and barrels from the supply ship, under the watchful eye of several guards. But as she stared at the sloping hull of the Apum-Ka, her world froze. For the space of a heartbeat, she saw only workers hauling crates up the steep incline, Koru-Kah guards standing watch. Even with her canes—she could never climb that slope. She would have to crawl, dragging herself past the strange, cruel Koru-Kah guards.

Her gaze shifted from the sloping gangway to Jacuti, who knelt, head bowed, before Captain Ki-Kuna and an older Koru-Kah leader — whose face was adorned with intricate tattoos. The inked designs ran down his neck and along his arms, ending in black shark teeth on the backs of his hands. The two men's faces bore striking similarities — father and son, perhaps.

The Koru-Kah leaders were talking, pointing at Kei. The heavily tattooed older man frowned, shook his head, and pointed at Kei again before flicking his hand toward the open ocean, chilling her.

"Tacheh keetuh," he said, flicking his hand at the water. Ki-Kuna bowed in acknowledgment, but before he could turn to carry out his father's orders, Jacuti prostrated himself, pressing his forehead to the deck and spreading his arms in front of him. His groveling submissiveness shocked Kei.

Captain Ki-Kuna struck Jacuti's shoulder with a wood cudgel, raising a welt. But Jacuti pressed his forehead harder into the deck, speaking rapidly to the Koru-Kah in their own language.

*"Ia he **Singer**, me tōku māmā, Namaua,"* Jacuti said, his words unintelligible to Kei, other than that one word: ***Singer.***

Both leaders looked again at Kei, a new interest in their eyes. The older leader shrugged, saying,

"Schrenku. Māhn!"

"Āe! Atūt-Mā!" Jacuti exclaimed, rising to his feet. He kept his head bowed as he turned and fled from the Koru-Kah

leaders, leaping into the boat's stern near Kei's tethered kayak and gathering up her canes. He then returned to Kei, saying:

"Thee must sing, Kei. Thee must sing fer the *Atūt-Mā* — the Great Ones — or they vill slay thee."

Jacuti pointed toward the dock but lowered his arm as a red flush bloomed on Kei's face — her only way off the boat was to crawl. Jacuti glanced at the Great Ones, who paid no attention, then turned his broad back to Kei, saying,

"Put thy armes about me."

Kei swallowed, understanding the unspoken message. She reached for Jacuti's shoulders. As her hands slid around his neck, she felt the scarred ribbons on his smooth skin — white, lumpy scars embossed by the lash of an Atūt-Mā on his sun-darkened flesh.

Her arms encircled Jacuti's shoulders and neck, clinging to him as she had when she was a child, carried on her father's strong back.

Jacuti straightened, lifting her with ease. He stepped onto the dock, and Kei realized just how large he was. The young man towered over the other workers — even the guards, who fingered their weapons as Jacuti carried her to a crate, setting her down as if she were a child.

"Sing a vorkin' song, Kei. Don't stop til the unloodin' is done."

The crate's splintered wood dug into her skin. Sunlight gleamed off the long knives of the guards, while the unblinking eyes of the Atūt-Mā crushed her, trapping her voice beneath their cruelty.

But Jacuti stood before her, nodding encouragement.

"Sing, Kei. Sing fer me." His eyes met hers, and his calloused hand began a rhythm, thumping a steady heartbeat against his muscled chest—just as her father had done for her so many times in Tirahanko Bay.

Thump. Thump. Thump.

Held safe in Jacuti's rhythm, Kei's mind soared freely. Her song poured out, flashing past the gleaming blades of her Koru-Kah guards, rising in time with Jacuti's heartbeat tempo. Drumbeats and soaring notes echoed over the docks and boats, carrying toward the emotionless Atūt-Mā—the "Great One" who held her life in his hands.

But Kei sang for Jacuti, her eyes locked on his.

With each strike against his sunburnt skin, Jacuti matched the rhythm of her song.

Do you see me as I am?
Swimming deep beneath the waves.

Voice and drumbeat entwined

If you see me as I am,
I will love you all my days.

Her voice reached its highest notes, and the melody filled the dock. The Koru-Kah turned to her as she sang. For the first time, she saw Captain Ki-Kuna smile. He could not understand her words, but she sang the language of music, and both Atūt-Mā responded.

For a moment, all motion on the docks ceased as captors and enslaved workers listened. But she did not sing to the Koru-Kah, she sang for Jacuti alone.

And when her final note faded, drifting out to sea, the branded workers shouldered their burdens once more, breaking the spell she had woven. Yet as they toiled past her, they smiled — grateful for the beauty and power of her voice.

The older Koru-Kah leader, Commander Té-Anka, stared at Kei from behind his tattooed face.

"*Tō maih. A ki tahn matua,*" he said to Jacuti, who translated for Kei: "*Take her to your mother. Teach her our songs.*"

Jacuti remained motionless, eyes locked on Kei, until a guard smacked a wooden club against the scars on his back, demanding that he return to work.

"Sing fer me vhile I vork," Jacuti said, light shining from his face as he turned away from her, "*Sing* for me, Kei."

And she did, lifting her voice in a working chant she once sang on the sandy beaches of Tirahanko Bay, where villagers — her family and friends — salted fish and repaired their hunting kayaks.

That world felt like another life. But here, on the Apum-Ka, her song belonged to Jacuti alone.

Oh Love, Through Tears

Kei and Jacuti stood atop the Apum-Ka's hull, beneath a blue-white dappled sky. Kei leaned into her canes, while Jacuti supported her with one arm wrapped around her shoulders. Enslaved workers trudged behind them, carrying supplies down a wooden ramp into the Apum-Ka's bowl-shaped interior. A Koru-Kah village sprawled there, on the giant raft's reed deck. Kei looked past the wooden forecastle rising above the hull to a bustling hive of workers swarming the deck, harvesting the sea.

On the opposite side of the Apum-Ka, suspended between two poles, a gigantic trawling net cascaded into the water, its length disappearing into the depths. A cold shiver ran down Kei's spine as she watched the massive trawling net, which must be the same kind that had torn through the coral gardens of the Kopri, dismembering and ruining the ocean floor. Her eyes flicked to the dock, where the harpoon boats were tied. A rush of revulsion rose in her chest. She knew what those boats were for: to tear through the oceans, killing whatever they could find — whales, fish, and even kopri. A sickening feeling washed over her at the thought of the Koru-Kah's callous destruction, indifferent to the lives they ravaged.

The image of the shattered kopri nest, where OldFish and DeepRunner had mourned the loss of so many younglings, surged within her, threatening to spill tears into her eyes. She leaned into Jacuti, his arm warm against her shivering skin. This Koru-Kah world — the strangeness of it. A hard lump formed in the back of her throat. She swallowed, then turned back to the busy dockyard sprawling at the base of the wooden ramp.

There, captive laborers sorted supplies and carried them to warehouses, under the baleful gaze of Koru-Kah guards.

"What did you say to the *Atūt-Mā*? To the *Great One*?" Kei asked.

"I told them thee could sing, like my muhter. And that thee could sing fer them — vhen she dies."

Kei glanced at the spiral brand on Jacuti's cheek, her voice dropping an octave lower in pitch. "What's wrong with her?"

"Nauthin'. But life is hard. Short." Jacuti's eyes closed for the space of one throbbing heartbeat. He pointed to the far side of the raft, at the twin posts projecting from the hull which held the trawling net. Teams of workers drew the net aboard, while fish of every size and shape flopped onto the Apum-Ka's reed deck, gasping out their lives. Other workers gutted the dying fish, packing filets in salt barrels to preserve the flesh.

"The *slawghtehr* — slaughter — deck. We vork there, every day. There is no rest," the young man said, pointing at the blood drenched reeds beneath the trawling net. His hand contracted into a fist, banging against his hip. Words became a growl in his throat, lips clenching, but he pushed his chest out, drawing in air before continuing, "Vhen vee grow sick, too old to vork, the *Atūt-Mā* trowe — throw — us into the sea. My muhter is old; only her voice keeps her alive."

"They'd really kill her? Kill me? If we can't sing or work?"

"Vee are possessions. *Na-manu* — less than human. If vee can't vork, they have no use fer us." Darkness haunted the spaces behind Jacuti's eyes. His nostrils widened, cheeks quivering with a lifetime's anger, carefully hidden from view. "But they value my muhter's voice. She sings fer them on the long floats between Koru-Kah harbors."

One of the guards shouted at Jacuti. His eyes lowered, all expression fleeing his face, shoulders slumping. But Kei saw a flicker of rebellion hidden behind his down-turned eyes. The powerful young man squatted, letting Kei wrap her arms around his neck and climb onto his broad back. The rope-like scars on his back pressed into Kei's chest, heat rising where their skin met.

He carried her down the ramp into a busy dockyard below the forecastle. From the command deck above, Koru-Kah leaders shouted orders, reinforced from time to time by the wooden clubs of impassive guards.

At the bottom of the ramp, Jacuti gently lowered Kei to the deck, which shifted with the motion of the waves. She leaned into her canes, taking several faltering steps on the tightly woven reed deck, marveling that the entire Apum-Ka was built of reeds. Serpentine bundles formed the hull, while square reed mats, wider than her kayak, were stitched layer on layer to form the main deck. Bamboo posts supported the thatched roofs of warehouses rising from the deck, with thin reed curtains for walls. The curtains kept out the rain but did little to block the wind — or the stench of death wafting from the slaughter deck. Wooden planks formed gangways in some areas, making walking easier, though most of the woven deck remained exposed.

The tips of Kei's canes pierced the weaving of the reed deck mats, each step came slowly.

"We vill make reed sandals for thy *cahnz*," Jacuti said, pointing at the thonged sandals worn by their guards. The wide flexible soles of the woven sandals spread the Guard's weight evenly across the reeds, keeping their feet from sinking into the deck mats. Kei watched the bare feet of the na-manu workers, whose heels sank into the reeds like her canes, while the guards strode over the reed mats, lashing out with their cudgels and shouting orders in their caustic language.

"My muhter vill make some for thy *cahnz* — thy *canes*."

"Why aren't you wearing sandals?" Kei asked.

"The guards vill not allow. Easier fer them to catch and vhip us vhenever they vant." Kei said nothing as Jacuti squatted on the deck. Silently, she wrapped her arms around his shoulders, letting him carry her again. She did not understand these people. These Koru-Kah, who would hobble workers to make it easier to whip them.

Jacuti wove through stacks of crates and barrels, carrying Kei into the shifting shadows beneath the towering forecastle. Above, voices rang out as Apum-Ka officers barked orders from the command deck. The forecastle loomed over the dockside, its wood plank walls stark against the reed-woven expanse of the lower decks—solid and immovable.

That is vhere the Koru-Kah live," Jacuti said, keeping his voice low to avoid drawing the guards' attention.

"How do they get up there?" Kei asked, her breath quickening, heat rising to her cheeks as she spoke in a hushed voice.

"A ladder, inside."

Kei looked around the dockyard, at the guards with their long knives and wood batons, and at the na-manu, who shuffled over the reed deck, branded faces downcast. Beaten. Defeated.

"Will they brand me too?" she whispered.

"Yah," Jacuti replied, "but naught 'til they decide to keep thee."

A shiver ran across her shoulders and down her spine.

What had DeepRunner gotten her into?

These Koru-Kah were not people! They were sharks who would devour her.

Kei shivered, clinging to Jacuti as he carried her past huts stacked with crates and barrels. Amid the storage buildings, a longhouse loomed at the Apum-ka's outer edge, encircled by a palisade of spike-tipped wooden poles. She tightened her grip on Jacuti's neck as he carried her toward the sturdy longhouse. Its simple wooden door was guarded by two Koru-Kah, cudgels and knives at their sides, whose stony gazes dared Jacuti to step out of line. His eyes narrowed as he stepped past them, head held high, and carried Kei into the longhouse — the prison he called home.

* * *

Three-foot swells rippled over the ocean, breaking in whitecaps against the Apum-ka's steep-sloped outer hull. Diamond light glinted from the swells, reflecting off one enormous kopri eye that extended like a snail's eyestalk, peering toward the edge of the Apum-ka.

OldFish's other eye remained below the surface, staring at DeepRunner, who floated beneath the waves, mantle gray and silent. Ridges swelled across OldFish's body; red anger blended with blue swirls of despair.

"The beasts have taken her," OldFish signed.

"It is what she came to do," DeepRunner flashed back.

"She came to sing, from the safety of her kayak. That is what you promised."

Gray smoothness was DeepRunner's only reply.

"We promised to keep her safe." OldFish's tentacles glowed a livid red, not pulsing with light and dark, but shining with a steady, angry brightness through the clear water.

Annoyance crisscrossed DeepRunner's mantle, lines of black and gray flashing rhythmically: *"Risk swims with all journeys. This is no different."*

"You lied to her."

"Did you think there was no danger? Did you think this journey would be as easy? We aren't hunting crabs in a shallow cove! You knew the danger. Did you tell her that? If I lied, then so did you." Purple pulsed across DeepRunner's body, black knobs rising and falling with command. DeepRunner rotated both eyes upward to OldFish, daring the smaller kopri to say more.

OldFish's skin drained of color, a flood of colorless white claiming innocence before it faded into melancholy blue, then deepened into the darkest black of mourning. Their eyestalks retracted, disappearing into the mantle, shutting out the world — and with it, any further conversation with DeepRunner, who seemed to care so little for Kei's life.

But OldFish cared. Pink phosphorescence suffused every inch of their body, glowing steadily with thoughts of Kei — lost on the floating island. Then, streaks of red and black flared across OldFish's mantle, a surge of regret and anger at themselves. Their eyes pushed upward, extending above the waves, as both eyestalks rotated, scanning the edges of the floating island, where whitecaps crashed impotently against the towering outer hull.

OldFish would watch. And wait. And listen for Kei's song above the waves.

* * *

The na-manu prison longhouse was as wide as seven kayaks and stretched fifteen long. A thatched roof covered only part of the enclosure, leaving the na-manu quarters exposed to wind and rain. Woven pallets lay scattered on the deck beneath the thatching. In the far corner, a reed privacy screen stood in front of a pit that pierced the deck of the Apum-ka—a board-covered latrine hole emptying into the sea.

Jacuti carried Kei to the center of the longhouse, where a group of older enslaved na-manu sat together, eating. The few words exchanged came in a jumble of different languages. Occasionally, a pair of na-manu might share the same tongue, but mostly they communicated through hand gestures and smiles. The Koru-Kah deliberately separated their enslaved workers by language, preventing them from conspiring together. Only his mother's value as a Singer—and Jacuti's role as her drummer—kept the Koru-Kah from separating them as well.

It was a greater privilege than most na-manu received.

An edible harvest from the sea was spread near the na-manu: sheets of dark green kelp, clusters of sea grapes, and a type of thin translucent seaweed Kei did not recognize. A pile of fresh raw fish lay on another mat, where younger na-manu took turns cutting succulent red flesh with the honed edge of a giant clamshell. The na-manu elders, none much older than Kei's own mother, sat hunched in their silent circle. Scars laced their slumping backs, sparing no one. The group ate without speech, eyes drained of light by weariness and time.

Just beyond the circle of quiet na-manu, a woman sat alone. Her cheeks, darkened to a burnt umber by decades of labor under a relentless sun, contrasted with the slender grace of her trembling hands—calloused fingertips betraying a lifetime of hard work.

Jacuti lowered Kei to the woven reed mat beside the older woman.

"Hello mama," Jacuti said, placing each word into the air with rhythms and tones that Kei easily understood. "The sea hath brought a gift"

Etched creases curved into a well-worn smile around the woman's warm eyes, drawing a smile in return from the strange girl her son had brought to meet her.

"Kei," Jacuti said, still assembling each word with care, "this is my muhter. Namaua. She is a Singer. Like thee."

"Aroha, Kei. Kahea teu hākú." Namaua smiled, greeting Kei in the language of the Koru-Kah. Her melodic voice held a questioning note. She glanced first at her son, then back at the young woman sitting beside her. Namaua's gaze dropped to Kei's canes, then to her rigid legs.

"Hello Namaua," Kei said. "I'm sorry. I don't understand." The woman's eyebrows arched upward, smoothing the wrinkles around her eyes in surprise.

"*Thee speakest the lahngvitch—*" Namaua shook her head, raising her voice an octave, "I mean, thee speak the language of the Nadako Sea. Oh child, what fate hath brought thee here?"

Kei heard the rhythm of her own village in the lyrical voice of Jacuti's mother. For a moment, it was as if her own mother's songs were there, too. Her breath caught, a tightness spreading through her chest as the image of her mother—singing on the black sand beach of Tirahanko Bay—swept over her, leaving an aching emptiness behind. Kei drew a long breath. She glanced at Jacuti, then back to the older woman.

"You are from the Nadako?" Kei asked.

"Yes." Shadow deepened in the wrinkled etchings around Namaua's eyes. "From Meransi, the Many Isles, on Nadako's southern edge. But so long ago. When I was young. Like thee." Namaua reached one hand to Kei's canes, veins lacing dark brown hands, sculpted by hard labor. She then tapped Kei's stiffened legs.

"Dost thee have a song? For this?" Namaua asked, a slight accent remaining in her voice. Kei stayed silent, looking away from the inviting smile of Jacuti's mother. When Kei said no more, Namaua nodded her head, body bowing.

"Sorrow remains forever," the older woman said, "unless we find a home for it. Jacuti says thee art a Singer. For Singers, like us, sorrow belongs in song."

Kei remained silent, but one hand clenched into a fist, dropping to her unresponsive thigh in the dimming light of approaching night.

"An accident." Kei said, unable to meet the older woman's eyes. "But I have no song."

"An accident. And now thee art here," Namaua replied. "Oh child, such sorrow for one so young."

Namaua closed her eyes, taking several breaths, and nodding toward her son.

Following his mother's cue, Jacuti put down his food, beginning a complex drumbeat on his chest.

A ripple of silence swept around the circle of eating na-manu. Decades of whips and bludgeoning rods lifted briefly from the drooping shoulders of the na-manu elders, who had few reasons for joy. Food was put down, and several aging men echoed Jacuti's rhythm on their own scarred chests. A woman, no older, but far more weary than Namaua, picked up a wooden spoon, rapping time against her plate.

In anticipation of their Singer's voice, all eyes and ears turned to Namaua, whose breathing slowed as she prepared to sing.

The thumping, clicking drumbeats continued, steady, a language all the Na-Manu listening understood. And Kei heard her father's voice:

"*All people share a drum,*" he once told her, thumping his fist against his heart, "*Music is a language known to everyone.*"

Gently, a melody rose into the air, an octave lower than any kopri could hear. Ache edged each note, melody raw and dripping with loss. Namaua sang in the language of the Nadako, and while most of the enslaved people sitting nearby could not understand her words, they heard the language of the drums and raw emotion, translated into melody and song as Nammau put her own bitter sorrow into song:

Koru-Kah lashes on the back of my love,
Who raced to set me free,
From tangled nets that dragged me deep,
To death's embrace at sea.

I see my lover turning,
Grabbing a hard Koru-Kah knife,
Slashing through the tangled lines,
My lover saves my life.

But as I lay there gasping,
The Koru-Kah raise him high,
They cast my love into the sea,
Through tears I watched him die.

They cast him out into the sea,
For the crime of saving me,
For the crime of saving me,
For the crime of saving me.

Namaua's voice dropped to a whisper. Silence filled the circle of gathered na-manu, victims of the Koru-Kah themselves. Jacuti placed a hand on his mother's shoulders.

"My fadder died before I vas born," he said. "The *Atūt-Mā* vould have killed my muhter too. Except for her voice." A frown tightened on Jacuti's lips. "They let her live because she knew their songs."

Stone lay behind Jacuti's gentle eyes. A hardness unseen by Kei before, as the kind young man thought about the father he never knew, killed by the Koru-Kah. Namaua turned her head, warming her son's hand with a mother's kiss as Jacuti closed his eyes.

Waves crashed against the outer hall of the Apum-ka, sending vibrations spiraling through the serpentine reeds of the raft. Wind blew down over the high spiked walls of the na-manu prison.

"My father left me," Kei said, breaking the silence with the sound of her own sorrow. Somehow, the strangeness of the na-manu prison removed the chains from her memories. "He crashed our kayak into the reef, then swam away. Saved himself. Left me to die."

Bitterness furrowed Kei's brow, not with sadness, but anger. Suppressed, unfelt — until this very moment.

"He left me to die. I didn't, but waves shattered my spine on the coral." Kei's jawline trembled, but no tears fell. The past was gone. She was here. Now. With neither her mother nor father to blame for the choices that had brought her to the Koru-Kah.

"But thee survived," Namaua said. Kei nodded.

"A kopri. My friend, OldFish, pulled me from the reef and has swum with me ever since."

"Kopri?" Namaua's eyes widened. "The kopri hear thee?"

"Yes," Kei replied, thinking little of that fact.

Jacuti frowned. Began to speak. But Namaua waved him silent, saying, "Jacuti, a Singer is more than a weaver of melodies on the wind. A true Singer can be heard by the Kopri. I've told thee about them."

"I thought it just a story. Talking octopus—?"

"The kopri are real!" Namaua replied, "I followed one named DeepRunner here. To save the Kopri."

"DeepRunner?" Kei asked, the name bursting from her lips in a heated rush. Namaua tilted her head, eyes narrowing as she looked at Kei.

"A young and fearless kopri with a scar beneath their eyes," Namaua said, "who came from the Menehko Ocean to Meransi, asking for a Singer to speak for the Kopri. I went with DeepRunner. And I sang to the Koru-Kah. But failed."

"DeepRunner is older than I thought," Kei whispered.

"Thou knowest DeepRunner?" Namaua leaned back, gripping Jacuti's hand.

"Yes. I came here with them."

Namaua squeezed her eyes shut. "And DeepRunner abandoned thee, too?"

Kei's tongue flicked over suddenly dry lips.

"No," she said. "I had a chance to escape. But I chose—I chose to come here. To the Apum-ka."

"Why, child?" Namaua asked.

"Because your son could speak with me. And I came to save the Kopri. I thought that Jacuti could help me *Sing* to the Koru-Kah. Make them understand."

"But DeepRunner left?" Namaua asked, bitterness souring her words.

"I don't know. But OldFish wouldn't leave me. Not my friend. I know OldFish is out there, listening, and will save me if I leap into the sea."

Tears appeared on Namaua's wrinkled cheeks. "Jacuti," she said, "a Singer and a kopri! This is thy chance."

Namaua gripped Jacuti's hand with all her strength, knuckles turning white, her accent thickening as she turned to Jacuti and exclaimed, "Thou canst be free!"

"Thou canst finally be free!"

Treasure of the Leaf

Rotting reeds hung suspended from the floating island's underside, where shrimp and crab and fish made a living in a world grown from Koru-Kah debris. The giant raft's reeds swelled in salt water, gradually decaying into tattered strands and falling to the bottom of the sea.

OldFish clung to the underside of the raft, weaving tentacles into clumps of dangling reeds, matching the raft's color and texture. Camouflaged, OldFish disappeared into the ecosystem below the Apum-ka's rotting bottom. Nearby, an air-filled shaft, wider than a kayak, pierced upward through the deck of the Apum-ka, ending in a bright blue disk of open sky. Where air met water in the shaft's bottom, Koru-Kah garbage rotted: fish guts and severed fish heads, whose bulging, horrified eyes stared forever at nets dragging them from the sea. The skin and bones tossed from the dry world above fed crab, shrimp and rainbow-colored baitfish, creating a habitat that existed nowhere else.

OldFish's beak crushed a crab, serrated tongue savoring and devouring the prey that had strayed too near the camouflaged kopri.

Weeks had passed with no sound of Kei, and OldFish's hopes had dimmed. DeepRunner threatened to depart, but OldFish shamed the surly kopri into staying.

"*She failed,*" DeepRunner said, aging tentacles blackening with despair. The long days of waiting for any sign of Kei hung heavy along the ancient kopri's drooping tentacles as they signed, "*Humans are useless.*"

OldFish's gray skin remained calm and smooth. "*We don't know that,*" OldFish signed. "*Give her more time.*"

"*Time!*" DeepRunner's mantle pulsated in a web of deep purple frustration. "*I have no time left.*"

Orange knobs rose in a ring around OldFish's eyes. Questioning.

"*I have swum this current since my earliest days.*" DeepRunner signed, "*Time. I have none. The Deep draws near for me. My quest will fail. And with me, all our younglings.*" Phosphorescent light on the ancient kopri's skin faded to a mottled black, drooping down tentacles and mantle.

"*How long have you sought the Koru-Kah?*"

"*A lifetime,*" DeepRunner replied, "*I quested with my Singer, Namaua, long before you hatched.*"

OldFish's eyes turned on DeepRunner, compassion lighting in the darkness, *"Then what are a few more risings of the sun? We can wait."*

"Humans!" DeepRunner's sign flared with rippling shafts of purple-red. *"They need to learn their place!"*

"Humans aren't prey."

"Aren't they?" DeepRunner asked, *"they shrivel after minutes below the waves."*

"We hunt together. They sing to you," Old Fish answered quickly.

"Yours do. From the inner sea. But these humans. The Koru-Kah." DeepRunner faded gray. *"They are wordless predators. Sharks. Barracuda."*

"Kei will sing to them!" OldFish asserted.

"I am tired of talking. In all the seasons I've talked, nothing has happened. And soon I will drop into darkness. The Deep comes for me."

DeepRunner's mantle shifted black, then red knobs rose in rings around protruding eyes. *"They are beasts. I should kill them. Like any shark stealing my prey."*

"What? You would hunt them?" Alternating rings of red and black disgust circled OldFish's eyestalks, which drew a steady red from DeepRunner — rage burning brighter and brighter.

"Yes." DeepRunner signed. *"They are just humans. Just useful prey. If they won't hunt for me, then I will take them with me to the Deep."*

OldFish's eyestalks bulged at DeepRunner, as the older kopri turned gray and jetted toward the edge of the Apum-ka, disappearing from view.

Currents flowed beneath the rotting reeds of the Apum-ka's underbelly. Crabs skittered from carcass to carcass, floating at the shaft's bottom. OldFish reached out a tentacle, seizing a crab. Then, unexpectedly, high, sweet tones echoed down the shaft.

After so many days, OldFish finally heard Kei's song, strong and clear.

The crab dropped from OldFish's tentacles, falling forgotten into the depths, as OldFish turned and jetted toward Kei's song, all despair forgotten.

* * *

A hundred tiny cuts from splintered reeds lacerated Kei's hands, slicing into palms and fingers that had grown calloused from two long weeks of weaving stalks into mats.

"Thy hands have hardened," Namaua said, reaching for another bundle, her fingers deftly weaving the reeds into a mat slowly taking shape within a circle of women too old, or too weak, to work the slaughter deck. Few words were spoken as they worked.

Bruise-colored clouds filled the sky, threatening rain with a wind which raised white crested water across the endless ocean. Younger na-manu worked the nearby slaughter deck, gutting and beheading fish that fell from a trawling net onto the red-stained reeds of the Apum-ka.

"Where will this mat be placed?" Kei asked, a bead of blood pricking from a fingertip, pierced by the splintered end of a reed woven into the mat's outer edge. The prick would heal, leaving behind a hardened layer of protective scar tissue.

"Beneath the supply huts, on the other side of the command deck," Namaua replied.

"Why are so many supply huts empty?" Kei asked absentmindedly as she wove.

"The Empire sends supplies to its western provinces. They're unloaded when the Apum-ka passes by the Koru-Kah's southern colonies, and replaced by gold, dried reeds and salt. We float north now, through the richest fishing grounds, weaving the stalks and filling the supply huts with salted fish to feed the Empire."

Namaua fell silent, her fingers flicking as she wove. Kei said nothing, trying to envision the vast world — the Koru-Kah Empire — that Namaua had described. Her simple village life felt distant, almost lost, overwhelmed by the titanic forces of the Koru-Kah.

"The weaving never stops," Namaua said. "Water rots the reeds. Everything falls off the underside with time. So we lay new reed mats and bundles, lashing them in place. Endlessly, or the Apum-ka would fall apart and sink."

Kei looked across the debris shaft — an open pit leading to the sea — to where Jacuti and a team of muscled na-manu hoisted ropes. A trawling net trailed behind the Apum-ka, as wide as seven kayaks.

The na-manu heaved on lines, ropes cutting into calloused palms, pulling the net in from the sea. Teams of workers faced away from the net, ropes lacerating their shoulders as they strained to spill the net's catch onto the bloodied slaughter deck. Watching Jacuti work, Kei realized again how much bigger he was than the other na-manu, easily handling twice as much load on the ropes as the other enslaved workers. No wonder the Koru-Kah valued him.

Namaua's voice broke through Kei's thoughts: "I've crossed the Menehko twenty times. Sixteen since Jacuti was born." The older woman's hands continued their deft work, but her eyes closed, tremors crossing her brows. "Its been so long," Namaua whispered, "since I left the islands of Meransi." She let out a weary sigh, then returned to her work before a Koru-Kah guard could notice her signs of weakness.

"How long does each cycle take?" Kei asked.

"The currents match the seasons. A full year."

"Twenty years," Kei whispered to herself. She glanced up from her weaving, at the command deck high above the working areas of the raft. There, the supply boat captain, Ki-Kuna, stood beside his father, Commander Té-Anka.

"Ki-Kuna would still have been a child when you arrived. Was Té-Anka the commander when you came?"

"No," Namaua replied. "The Koru-Kah change with the years. They come. They go. But the work remains."

"So the Koru-Kah you sang to, about the Kopri. Are any of them still aboard?"

"No. This is Té-Anka's first season commanding the Apum-ka."

"Maybe he would listen?"

"I doubt it. I tried, year after year. Changing my song for each new commander, but no one ever listened."

Kei's brows knit in thought as she asked, "But not this one? You haven't tried with Té-Anka?"

"No. There's no point to it. Thee knowest them naught, Kei. You couldn't. Nothing like the Koru-Kah exists in our Nadako Sea. They will not listen."

"I have to try. You said you composed a song in their language. Teach it to me."

"Thee shouldst think about escape!" Namaua exclaimed, fear tinging her words, "while thy kopri friend is still near."

Thoughts of escape flickered through Kei's mind. She longed to agree. To slip over the side of the giant raft into the embrace of her dear friend, OldFish, and make the long journey home. To sit atop the NetSinger's platform in Tirahanko bay. To sing with her mother's choir, just one of many voices, joined in harmony. Even to argue again with her father. Or better, to listen to his intricate rhythms on the sea drums in Tirahanko Bay.

She ached to go home. But—

"Not until I try," Kei said, her voice firm with resolve, "The Koru-Kah *heard* me when I sang on the docks, the day I arrived. They responded to my melodies. I must try. For the Kopri."

Namaua's hands did't falter. She wove reed into reed, the sharp splinters unable to pierce decades of thick dead skin built-up on her hands. *Perhaps,* Namaua allowed herself to think, *perhaps Kei can reach them.*

"Not all of them are evil," Namaua whispered, her mind lost for a moment in the memory of a handsome young Koru-Kah officer. But that was eighteen long years ago, and so she shook the memory away, focusing again on Kei.

"For thine sake, and Jacuti's, I will teach thee. But thee must make me a promise."

The two women wove reeds while Namaua composed her thoughts. Then her eyes glinted, face hardening as she spoke.

"Thee must promise, whether or not the Koru-Kah listen. Thee and thy kopri friends shall take Jacuti home to the Nadako Sea."

"I will," Kei said, without a moment's hesitation.

Namaua sought truth in Kei's eyes. Then she nodded. And began singing her song, the Koru-Kah words rising into the air.

"*Atūt-Mā, schrehtani hakinneh. Schrehtani hekeh.*" She sang, repeating Nadako words after each line, "*Great one, hear my song. Hear my plea.*"

With her gifts as a Singer, Kei quickly learned the words of Namaua's song.

And though the melody was perfect, she heard the haughtiness of DeepRunner in the notes, not the anguish of a father grieving at the grave of a shattered kopri nest.

"How would I say, *'our younglings starve'* in the words of the Koru-Kah," Kei asked.

Namaua sat for a moment, eyes downcast, lips moving silently. Then she sang softly, combining Kei's words in counterpoint to her own harmony, in the language of the Koru-Kah.

Kei nodded, then spoke another line. Together, Kei and Namaua blended their songs, replacing the commandments of the younger DeepRunner with the grief of that ancient Kopri's final days. Together, Kei and Namaua composed a new song.

A song for the children of the Kopri.

When the song was complete, and Kei had memorized each new line, she sang alone, allowing her voice to spill over the reed mats of the Apum-ka. Her melody fell into the gaping mouth of the debris pit—where a na-manu woman tossed the remains of some hapless fish, gutted on the Apum-ka's slick slaughter deck.

Before the last stanza passed her lips, however, a great shout rose from the trawling nets.

Guards pointed as a dark, man-shaped lump fell from the net onto the slaughter deck. The Koru-Kah guards swarmed the nets, pushing their enslaved na-manu away, allowing none to touch the treasure pulled from the sea.

Captain Ki-Kuna rushed from his high command post, joining a fiercely tattooed Koru-Kah Shaman at the side of the waterlogged prize. There, two baby kopri clung mindlessly to the body of a leafperson, feeding on a blue fungus that sprouted from every inch of its decaying flesh. This strange blue fungus — the Koru-Kah's greatest treasure — grew only here, in the warm mineral currents that flowed over the kopri spawning grounds.

* * *

Beneath the Apum-ka, OldFish continued to hear Kei's voice, faint and distant. It vibrated down the air-filled shaft, carrying strange words.

OldFish dropped the half-eaten crab clutched in their tentacles, and jetted toward the shaft — just as a butchered tuna carcass plunged into the water, where it bobbed among scraps unworthy of the Koru-Kah's storage barrels. The kopri ignored the carcass, raising an ear knob above the surface, straining to hear Kei's song.

OldFish's mantle flushed pink in a sudden rush, love blooming across their skin as Kei's voice echoed down the shaft.

"T'kopri tutacheh te," came the song, the clipped Koru-Kah words somehow made melodious by Kei's sweet voice.

The Koru-Kah words held no meaning for OldFish, but after so many days, hope had nearly faded — but now, hearing Kei's voice, the currents of the future flowed once more. Purple knobs flared around their eyestalks, which broke the water's surface, stretching toward the sliver of blue sky at the top of the air-filled shaft. Determination pulsed through OldFish's body, their tentacles pressing against the shaft's bundled reed walls, reaching, longing—climbing upward to Kei.

* * *

A strong wind pushed from the south, heavy with moisture and the clean scent of ocean brine. Guards formed a tight ring around the leafperson carcass, while a Koru-Kah Shaman, robed in bright red, knelt beside it. Kei stared across the open debris pit, watching Captain Ki-Kuna, who stood a few paces apart from the Shaman and the guards. As the Shaman led the Koru-Kah in a chant of praise to whatever vile gods they worshiped, the Captain remained silent, arms crossed, eyes sharp and locked on the carcass. Every movement, every shift in the air, seemed to be measured by his watchful gaze.

After completing the ritual chant, the crimson-robed Shaman thrust a dagger into one of the kopri younglings, which quivered, then lay limp on the blade. Another thrust, and the second youngling died. Then, slice by slice, the Shaman carefully cut mottled blue fungus from the leafperson's spongy body, being careful not to touch the fungus with his hands.

Above, the darkening clouds clumped together, pregnant with rain that refused to fall, filling the air instead with an oppressive moisture that beaded on Kei's forehead. But she ignored the discomfort, having grown used to adversity after these weeks laboring for the brutal Koru-Kah. Her eyes narrowed, focusing on the Shaman, who stacked sheaves of the precious blue fungus in a wooden chest. Beside the box lay the limp bodies of the two kopri younglings, slaughtered so casually by the Shaman.

"What are they doing?" Kei whispered, voice weeping at the murder of the younglings.

"Harvesting *Tayjaru*." Namaua replied. "A mushroom. Used to worship their gods. It only grows on dead leafpeople found here, in this one part of the ocean."

Kei looked across the reed deck at the leafperson's frail form. Vaguely human in shape, there was no head, only a trunk-like body with decaying wings sprouting from its back, thin and leaf-like, laying flaccid against the deck.

"What are they like," Kei asked, "the Leafpeople?"

"I've never seen one alive," Namaua replied, "Only dead ones like this, or flying high above, soaring from the slopes of Mt. Urkpry, near the southern harbors. Far to the south, there are often dead ones in the water. But the *tayjaru* grows on them only here."

"*Tayjaru*." Kei repeated, pulling her eyes away from the pitiful bodies of the younglings and focusing on the blue fungus growing on the leafperson. "What does it mean?"

Namaua frowned, searching for the right words. "*Giver of Mind*," she finally said. They believe eating it grants them power from their gods." She paused, her gaze shifting leftward in thought. "They take it in times of crisis, and during their rituals. I've been told that *Tayjaru* sharpens their minds—it keeps them awake and helps them notice patterns and connections they'd usually miss."

"So it makes them smarter?"

"Not exactly," Namaua said, shaking her head. "It doesn't give anyone knowledge they don't already have, but it helps people see things more clearly—connections, solutions, truths that were right in front of them. It lets people understand ideas they might have struggled with before."

Kei looked past Namaua to the Shaman, who continued harvesting the last remnants of blue fungus from the decaying leafperson carcass. As she watched, Captain Ki-Kuna reached around the Shaman, his arm brushing past him to lift the slain kopri younglings, who dangled limply in his iron grip.

Namaua followed Kei's gaze, her eyes heavy with sorrow. "It makes them smarter," she murmured, "but it doesn't make them wiser."

The Shaman finished his work, closing the lid of his storage box before rising to lead the Koru-Kah in a series of blessings and chants, their words unintelligible to Kei.

"*Tayjaru*," Kei whispered. "*Giver of Mind.*"

Then she sucked in a sharp breath and fell silent. Something shifted at the edge of her vision. There! In the debris shaft—an eyestalk thrusting up into the air! A kopri eyestalk, staring at the limp bodies of the two younglings swaying in Captain Ki-Kuna's uncaring grip.

OldFish!

Her friend's eye swiveled rapidly from the dead younglings to Kei, and back again. Before Kei could react, the chanting ceased, and the officers—now joined by Commander Té-Anka—began making their way back to the command deck.

Kei watched them approach, her gaze locked on the two lifeless kopri infants swinging in Ki-Kuna's grasp.

The Shaman passed by, followed by Commander Té-Anka, who stopped beside Namaua and Kei. His guttural words fell onto the deck, harsh and mingling with the blood of the murdered younglings:

"*Thee will sing tonight.*" Namaua translated.

Then Commander Té-Anka turned his gaze from Namaua to Kei, adding, "*Ah-en tureba—*" Namaua's translation chilled Kei's heart, "*Bring her. We will see if she is worth keeping.*"

When the last of the Atūt-Mā masters passed by, Kei sought OldFish's eye. But the horrified kopri had already fled to the safety of the sea—carrying the image of the slaughtered children with them.

Lost Upon the Water

Commander Té-Anka and the Shaman had long since left the slaughter deck. The sun now dipped toward the western horizon, spilling shades of orange, red, and purple across the cloud-filled sky—but still, the rain refused to fall.

Kei lingered near the debris shaft, hoping OldFish would return, but her friend never reappeared. Teams of workers carried barrels filled with salted fish to the supply huts, while Jacuti labored with several other na-manu, turning a screw pump, raising water up over the hull of the Apum-ka. The water ran down a sluice, filling a large cistern at the edge of the slaughter deck. Other enslaved na-manu filled buckets from the cistern, flinging salt water over the deck, cleansing whatever gore had not soaked into the mats. Pink-tinged slurry flowed across the red-stained reeds, washing fish guts down the debris shaft.

Soon, the cleanup was complete, and with the day's work done, the Na-manu began washing slick filth from their bodies.

Jacuti drew clean saltwater from the cistern, scrubbing slime from his arms and hands. Kei had joined him, her legs stiff and one hand pressed against the water tank to keep herself steady. Her other hand splashed saltwater across her skin, which burned from a hundred tiny pinpricks. The slaughter deck stretched before her, stained red. A sigh broke past her lips as she turned to Jacuti, whose long black hair hung damp in the sea breeze.

"How do you stand the itching?" She asked, "Don't you ever wash the salt away?"

Jacuti thought for a moment, before replying, "fresh water is too precious. Fer drinking only. Even the Atūt-Mā wash with salt water," he paused, frowning. "But when we filled the casks in Ar-Kora harbor with fresh water, I washed the sea away." The young man sighed, closing his eyes in blissful memory.

Jacuti drew a bucket of water from the cistern and poured it over his head for a final rinse. Water trickled over the web of scars lacing the young man's back. Kei reached out, tracing one of the puckered white ribbons snaking across his shoulder blade. Her gaze softened as her touch lingered on the bitter lumps rising in uneven knots from his abused skin.

"So many wounds," Kei murmured, her voice thick with emotion. "Why?"

Many na-manu bore the marks of Koru-Kah lashes on their backs, but Jacuti's flesh was more heavily scarred than most. He turned his head, reaching back to pull her hand from his skin, then turned toward her, holding her hand in his own.

"There is nowhere to run. Nowhere to escape," he said, his voice darkening. "But sometimes — I don't obey."

A shadow passed over his eyes. "Sometimes — I think I'd rather die than keep obeying. But I'm worth too much to kill. So they beat me instead."

A tremor rippled through Kei's lips and down her arm, where Jacuti's warmth pressed against her skin. Surprised, she realized she no longer noticed his accent, nor had any trouble understanding his words. Still, the heat of his body stirred something inside her — an ache for connection, unfamiliar and unsettling, like a longing she hadn't known she'd been missing.

Jacuti closed his eyes, his hand tensing, but when he opened them again, Kei found their depths full of warmth.

"But now," Jacuti said, "Thou art here."

Tingling filled her hand, and Kei kept her eyes locked on his steady gaze.

"Yes," she whispered, an inexplicable tightness spreading in her chest, the feeling too deep to define.

"When thee sing," Jacuti continued, "I hear the storm rising. But also —" the young man turned his head, breaking their eye's embrace as he furrowed his brows, looking at the Koru-Kah guards. His voice dropped. A hush came over him as he spoke, whispering, "Under their whips, I almost gave up. But now —"

His eyes returned to her face, their melodies merging as he repeated, "but now — thy kopri friends are here."

A storm surged through Kei's body as he spoke, but it quickly swept away as his words turned from her.

"I am not *na-manu*," the scarred young man said, certainty gleaming in his eyes with the last of the setting sun.

"I am Jacuti! And I will be free!"

* * *

That night, beneath the rising moon, Kei, Jacuti, and Namaua stepped into the Commander's mess hall—now transformed into a ritual chamber. Scented smoke swirled from embers glowing in braziers, each set into a wide, flat stone in the room's four corners. At the center of the chamber, the Koru-Kah Shaman stood before a crimson-stained wooden altar, leading the senior officers in a chant to their unknown gods as he poured a bowl of thick, red blood onto the vile shrine. Kei and Namaua took their seats while Jacuti stood nearby, beside a tall, upright drum.

Kei gagged on iron-rich smoke biting into her throat. Her dry lips quivered, as if she were watching a shark's fin circle her kayak. The Shaman's voice droned—off-key, rasping words void of meaning. There was no melody to the chant, only a monotonous buzz that raised the hairs on her neck and shivered down her spine, as if the shark's fin crept closer.

The shaman's words carried no kindness—only power and contempt.

How could she reach the shriveled hearts of these cruel Koru-Kah? She wanted to cry, but the dry smoke wicked every drop of moisture from her eyes.

Commander Té-Anka, his son Captain Ki-Kuna, and four lower-ranked officers sat on low cushioned stools, facing the Shaman. After completing the ritual, the Shaman took a seat across from the Commander, who barked an order to the na-manu servants waiting near the door.

A beautiful young na-manu woman glided to Té-Anka's side, kneeling with her head bowed. To Kei's eyes, she appeared exotic, with pale white skin and thick red hair that curled over her shoulders. The commander grinned, twisting his fingers in her long strands and pulling her closer. The woman winced but showed no other emotion, her soft eyes darkening with a sorrow that dulled their light.

Behind the woman, other servants stepped forward, carrying low tables which they placed before each Atūt-Mā. More na-manu entered, bearing a feast of choicest shellfish, tubers harvested from the land, and luxurious sweet honey paired with fresh unleavened bread. Laughter rang out in rough jests around the circle of feasting masters. Commander Té-Anka barked again, this time at Namaua, ordering her to sing an epic Koru-Kah ballad.

Jacuti began a hypnotic bass staccato on his drum, pounding out the harsh, martial rhythm favored by his captors. As the beat reverberated through the room, Namaua's voice rose in brutal koru-kah stanzas, singing of victory and slaughter in the far corners of the world.

Kei did not understand the words, but Namaua had told her that the Koru-Kah loved epic ballads of their vast empire's glory. The Koru-Kah language grated cruelly, but in Namaua's care, simple melodies infused the rasping lyrics, accented by the *boom-boom-boom* of Jacuti's palms striking leather stretched tight across his drum.

Kei followed the song, trying to memorize the words as her eyes flicked around the chamber. The incense rising from the braziers thinned, leaving behind an acrid sweetness in the air. The Atūt-Mā ate with their fingers, servants continually replenishing their plates. Meanwhile, lower-ranked officers vied for their commander's attention, trading jests at one another's expense. But Commander Té-Anka remained silent, appearing to listen to Namaua's songs. From time to time, Té-Anka glanced at Kei, speculation glinting in his hooded eyes. Beside her, Jacuti's gaze flicked between the commander and his mother, his brow furrowed in a deepening frown. A thought struck Kei, unbidden and unwelcome — what would happen to Namaua once she had passed down all her songs?

The Koru-Kah discarded all things they did not need.

The red-haired woman fed Commander Té-Anka morsels from her own hands, but he treated her as nothing more than a tool — something to be used and discarded at his whim. Namaua sang a dozen songs before the feast ended and servants cleared the tables. The pale woman knelt before the

Commander, pressing her forehead to the reed deck. Té-Anka grunted an order, dismissing the beautiful na-manu — his possession — with a twisted smile that left a queasy ache in Kei's stomach.

"*Uscht!*" Commander Té-Anka barked, ordering Namaua to stop singing. Silence swept over the room and the Koru-Kah officers turned to the Shaman, waiting.

The Shaman rose, carrying a gleaming gold tray, his voice droning in an endless chant as he returned to the stained wooden pedestal at the chamber's center. The grating monotone burrowed into Kei's ears as he set the tray upon the altar and unwrapped an oiled package. When he turned back to the officers, slivers of blue *tayjaru* fungus lay in his hands — harvested from the leafperson's body. Most were no larger than a fingertip, though two matched the size of a man's thumb.

The Shaman stood before a low-ranked officer.

"*Watatachi garuh?*" The Shaman's voice rang out, the words meaningless to Kei, but she listened intently, trying to grasp the ritual unfolding before her.

"*N'watachi ome!*" the officer responded, his tone ritualistic. Then, the Shaman placed a sliver of *tayjaru* into the man's mouth. Moving around the circle, the Shaman repeated the call-and-response with each officer. When he reached Commander Té-Anka, the ritual shifted. The Shaman handed the two remaining large slivers of blue fungus to Té-Anka, who took control of the ritual.

"Watatachi garuh?" the Atūt-Mā asked the shaman. Kei's lips moved as she tried to translate, having learned enough over the past weeks to guess at the meaning of the ritual words: "Are you worthy?"

"N'watachi ome! — I am worthless, enlighten me!" the Shaman responded, accepting a chunk of fungus from his master's fingers.

Té-Anka placed the remaining piece of fungus into his own mouth, chewing slowly and swallowing before sitting back on his low stool.

"Schrenku — Sing!" He called to Namaua, who lifted her voice in song. The older woman had prepared Kei for this part of the ceremony. The notes she sang carried no meaning, only a hypnotizing melody weaving through the scented smoke of incense. The song carried Kei along with it, and Jacuti beat a slow rhythm on his drum. Other than the music, no other sound rose from within the room. But howling wind and the distant crash of waves struck the Apum-ka's hull, sending echoes through the chamber. The sickly smoke curled in her throat and nostrils, stinging her eyes.

Soon it would be her time to sing! What had made her think she could do this? If only she could return to her mother's choir.

But there was no escape.

Kei kept her eyes blank when the Shaman shivered, a mirthless smile slicing over his face. Each of the officers seemed to stare into nothing, their eyes brightening, pupils expanding in the dim light as their minds raced.

Commander Té-Anka remained motionless, fixated on Namaua as the *tayjaru* took effect. His expression sharpened, his features tightening with sudden clarity. His eyes grew unnaturally bright, the pupils dilating until only black remained. A wicked grin stretched across his face as his mind raced, his gaze flicking around the room. He absorbed every detail, seeing connections and patterns he hadn't noticed before, as if the fog in his mind had cleared. *Tayjaru* heightened his intellect, making him more aware, more perceptive — and infinitely more dangerous.

Uscht — Stop!" he ordered, and Namaua fell silent. Té-Anka's eyes shifted to Kei, the razor-sharp gaze of a striking osprey fixing on her.

"Wa mascht ina," he commanded, a sharp motion of his hand signaling Kei to stand and sing. The words fell senseless on Kei's ears, but she knew it was finally time to prove her worth. If she failed, the relentless waves of the open ocean would be her reward.

Kei stood, balancing on her canes, showing no fear. An image of DeepRunner filled her mind — the ancient kopri so calm and deadly blue, embracing the crocodile without fear. Inspired by DeepRunner's courage, Kei refused to kneel before these horrible men. She would face them, on her own terms.

Té-Anka grinned.

"Schrenku — Sing!" he commanded, his bright eyes drilling into her soul.

The first koru-kah song she had memorized spilled from her lips, a Koru-Kah favorite, telling of heroic love and loss, which Namaua had taught her. Jacuti's drum stayed silent, allowing the strength of her voice alone to prove her worth. The commander leaned back on his stool, motionless, yet intent on every note. Kei's next song was in her own language, a tale of the hunt, a tale of kopri and humans working together. For that song, Jacuti struck a quiet rhythm on his drum.

Confusion clouded the lower-ranked officer's eyes, their gazes flickering as they leaned forward, but they masked their lack of understanding. Their smaller doses of *tayjaru* had sharpened their awareness just enough to sense something, but not enough to truly comprehend her Nadako words. Meanwhile, the Shaman and Té-Anka, who had taken larger doses, remained still, their eyes sharp and focused, as if the words Kei sang had been laid bare before them.

She sang two more Koru-Kah ballads, the martial rhythms pounding through the room like a heartbeat, and then her moment arrived—the reason she had journeyed from the safe waters of the Nadako Sea: to sing for the Kopri. Kei's voice fell silent. Distant crashing waves echoed in the chamber. Then, her voice rose, breathing life into the new song she and Namaua had composed together—a song of grief, hope, and a longing for peace. The song on which the hopes of the Kopri now depended.

"*Atūt-Mā, schrehtani me,*" Kei sang, her voice flowing in the slurred staccato rhythms of the Koru-Kah language. As the words left her lips, her mind simultaneously translated the lyrics into her own language.

"Great one, hear our song."
Your trawling nets destroy our world
Our children starve. Their minds grow dim
Raise up your nets that catch and smash
Atūt-Mā, let our peoples swim as one."

The song continued, recounting the lives of the Kopri, their love for one another. And the despair of shattered kopri nests and tiny graves forlorn beneath the waves. The song begged the Koru-Kah to hunt together with the Kopri, for their two peoples to swim together as one.

Can you see us as we are?
Swimming deep beneath the sea,
Please see us as we are
A people, strong and free.

Her voice fell into silence, and all eyes remained fixed on her. Hope swelled with each rise and fall of her chest.

But then Té-Anka laughed — a deep, brutal sound that filled the room with dark amusement.

"Kopri mata tureba!" he called to a servant, never taking his razor-sharp gaze from Kei.

Moments later, the servant returned, setting a covered crock on the mat in front of the Commander. Té-Anka smiled at Kei, flicking the lid off and plunging his hand into the preserving brine.

Laughing, he withdrew the contents, holding it out to Kei. The sight sent a dry heave through her stomach.

His laughter echoed, swirling around Kei, until Té-Anka spoke — his words slipping into the language of Nadako.

"Ai see thee ast thee art," he chuckled, taking a bite of the kopri youngling he held, slurping its soft tentacle into his mouth. The Atūt-Mā chewed, savoring the kopri's tender flesh, then handed the pitiful body to the Shaman.

Commander Té-Anka swallowed, cleared his throat, and spoke, his voice cutting through the silence.

"I see thee. As thee are," he said, derision lacing his words. *"You. Are. Prey."*

The Awakening

Namaua's voice wove through curling incense thickening the air, but Kei's world narrowed to the tiny youngling's carcass — its mantle and beak discarded like refuse on the floor. Ki-Kuna, the captain who had captured her, laughed as he kicked the ravaged youngling into the ghostly shadows pooling at the chamber's edge. Kei's vision constricted. Her world collapsed into this single moment, this single place. Every choice that had led her here — every decision made under the illusion that she could reason with the Koru-Kah, that they shared her humanity — mocked her now. Failure coiled through her muscles, clinging to her vision like cobwebs and souring her stomach with a burning pain.

She shrank away from the Koru-Kah and their *tayjaru*-brightened eyes, wishing she had never come to this place. Wishing she could be home, safe in her father's arms, hearing her mother's voice just one more time.

Lost in her longing, despair washed over her. She trembled, sinking to the floor—small and still—waiting for the pain to pass.

With a final, unintelligible ritual, the Shaman called the ceremony to a close, and the officers rose, seeking their beds. Namaua told Kei that the officers would sleep off the effects of *tayjaru* for days. The leafperson fungus exacted a heavy price for the keenness of mind it offered, and was rarely used, except in times of crisis.

The ceremony this night had been an exception: a reward from Commander Té-Anka for the wealth of fungus harvested from the decaying leafperson body.

Namaua left the chamber first, her eyes heavy with exhaustion. She sought sleep, leaving Jacuti and Kei to make their way back to the na-manu quarters. Kei allowed Jacuti to guide her, stumbling with each step, her feet dragging as she leaned on him for support.

Prey. She thought. We are just *prey* to them.

The warmth of Jacuti's arm wrapped around her shoulder, but her mind blazed with only one thought: *the Koru-Kah were worse than sharks.* Sharks, at least, ate only what they needed. The Koru-Kah plundered everything they touched, feasting on the world.

Kei understood that now. Clearly. Her foolishness—thinking she could change their minds—slammed into her like a tidal wave, driving her into the hard sand beneath a raging surf.

Midway between the Officers' Quarters and the na-manu prison compound, Kei's fingers tightened on her canes, trying to squeeze away the world. She stumbled on the undulating mats of the Apum-ka, sagging into her canes. Jacuti's arm tightened around her shoulder, holding her up, but even the warmth of his gentle hand supporting her could not cut through the chill freezing her heart.

Kei wrenched herself free from his hold, her fingers digging into her palms as she gripped her canes with all her strength.

She could feel Jacuti's gaze on her, but she kept her eyes forward, unable to face him. His focus never wavered, though she felt the weight of his concern as his eyes traced shadows carved by moonlight beneath her sorrowful eyes, trying to understand the depths of her turmoil. What could she possibly say to this gentle young man whose life she had entered like an osprey plummeting into a storm-tossed sea?

The Apum-ka's lookout mast rose above Kei and Jacuti, casting a long shadow in the moonlight. Her eyes followed its length as it stretched over the reeds, the shadow ending near the slaughter deck, where the scent of partially dried blood thickened the air. The stench clung to each breath, dragging memories from the depths of her mind — the half-eaten kopri youngling, Commander Té-Anka's smirk as he chewed and swallowed.

Kei's stomach churned, bile rising sharp and bitter in her throat as tears slipped down her face. Beside her, Jacuti stood helpless. He tried again to take her hand, but she waved him away, ashamed.

"Kei," he said, but she only tightened her grip on her canes and moved away.

The deck shifted beneath her, throwing her off balance. Her thighs and calves tensed, muscles straining to keep her upright—but failed. She crashed onto the deck, her canes clattering against the damp reeds that struck her face. Sobs tore from her bruised lips, tears spilling onto the woven reeds of the Apum-ka. Waves of grief washed over her—sorrow for the kopri youngling, bitterness at the loss of her legs, and a deep yearning to be in her mother's arms, lulled to sleep by her mama's voice.

She sobbed as wave after wave of despair rolled over her.

Jacuti lowered himself to the deck beside her, but kept apart. Waiting.

Kei's sobbing slowed as the mast's shadow stretched over the deck. Her tears dried—though grief remained, hidden deep beneath every breath she drew.

"My father told me—" her voice came thick with tears. She swallowed hard, gripping her canes like they were the only thing holding her together.

Jacuti hesitated. "Told thee what?"

Kei let out a bitter breath, the memory crashing over her. "That I quit, after the wreck. That I just gave up. That I stopped fighting." Her throat clenched. "And I hated him for it. Hated him for saying it. But he was right. I thought he was the one who gave up—crawling into his pipe, never coming out. But I did the same thing, didn't I?"

Kei let out a hollow laugh, raw and jagged. "We both gave up."

Jacuti's voice was soft, uncertain. "But he loved thee?"

Kei looked up at him, blinking back tears as memories of her father flooded her mind—his hands laboring to build outriggers for her kayak and his concern for her safety. With each memory, her anger toward him ebbed away, leaving behind the warmth of his embrace and the steady beat of his drums echoing in her heart.

"He did," she said, face trembling as she lifted it from the reeds.

Rolling onto her side, she stared up at Jacuti, his face softly lit by starlight. "I'm sorry," she murmured, her voice breaking slightly.

"For what?"

Kei's breath caught. "Even after he turned to smoke, my father loved me. I know that now." She paused, her throat tight. "But your father—you never knew him, did you?"

"No," the young man replied, "But I know he loved me."

"Yes, he would of," Key said, lost for a moment in Jacuti's kind eyes.

"No." Jacuti said, pressing his lips together, his voice slipping back into an uneasy accent. "Mine fadder died fer me. Fer me unt mine muhter." A tremor passed through his sunburnt lips, but certainty formed each word.

A milky white twinkling spread across the sky above. Beneath those endless heavens, Jacuti's voice reached to her, somehow a lifeline that drew her from her own despair.

"He knewst mine muhter car'd me," Jacuti said, "Knewst not jus' her, but his child dost save, vhen he grabbed a Koru-Kah blade and cutted her fromst da net."

"They killed him for saving Namaua?" Kei asked, her breath steadying as anger began to replace the anguish in her heart.

"No," Jacuti replied, bitterness slipping from his lips. "They kilt him fer touching the blade he used ta free her."

Kei sat up, reaching out to take Jacuti's hand.

"But he did it to save a pregnant woman! They're evil! The Koru-Kah. All of them!"

"Not all." Jacuti's voice softened. "Many only stay von season onst the Apum-ka. They don't like what they see. But the *Atūt-Mā* hold all the power."

He turned his head, unable to meet her eyes. A tremor passed through him, and for a moment, words stuck in his throat. A long, slow sigh escaped his lips, pushing the words out with it.

"Not all of them are evil," he said gently, "Not all."

He stopped speaking, a tremor passing his lips. But then, reluctantly, a buried thought escaped: "my father was Koru-Kah."

And there it was, his secret hanging between them. Slowly, he withdrew his hand, but Kei tightened her grip, refusing to let go. Their hands remained clasped.

"My father was a Koru-Kah officer," Jacuti began, his voice quiet but steady. "He fell in love with Mama and tried to escape with her—to free her. But they caught him. Made him na-manu as punishment. And later, when he took a weapon to save me and my muhter, they killed him."

Warmth passed between their hands, a silent exchange of comfort. In Jacuti's eyes—his Koru-Kah eyes—Kei saw her own father clearly for the first time. The two sides of him: a child's invincible protector, and the flawed man who loved her.

For a time, only the crashing of waves filled the silence, the weight of their shared sorrow hanging in the air. But the reality remained— they were prisoners, slaves of the Koru-Kah.

"A friend once told me," Kei said, thinking of OldFish, "That sometimes storms just come. It's no one's fault."

She released Jacuti's hand and grabbed her canes, struggling to her feet.

"A storm is no one's fault," she repeated, "but how we choose to paddle. That is our own choice."

"I am not prey," Kei said, turning to face Jacuti, who rose and stood beside her. "I can't change the Koru-Kah, but I can still keep the promise I made to your mother. My kopri friends are near. We can finish what your father started."

Kei's fingers tightened on her canes as she pushed doubt from her mind. "We will set you free. Both of us. Together."

* * *

OldFish waited at the bottom of the debris shaft. Was that Kei's voice? Distant? Too far away to risk climbing up the pit? OldFish waited beside the star lit opening, but Kei never came near. Dejected, OldFish finally turned and headed in the direction DeepRunner had swum, staying close to the decaying reeds of the Apum-ka's bottom, as it rose and fell on ocean swells. Water rippled around OldFish's serpentine tentacles as the kopri jetted toward a vibration pulsing through the lightless black brine.

DeepRunner clung in darkness to the bottom of the Apum-ka, mantle and tentacles throbbing phosphorescent red. The enormous kopri burrowed tentacle tips into the raft's reed cables, hard beak rasping across the fibers, digging, tearing, sending strands of reeds to the bottom of the sea. Black-blue ripples of exhaustion alternated with crimson rage on DeepRunner's mantle, but the ancient kopri worked on, sharp beak plunging into the woven cables. Over and over and over.

OldFish floated to a stop, their saddened blue mantle unseen by DeepRunner, whose rasping beak sent shivers through the water. Shredded reeds floated like a cloud around the older kopri. OldFish reached out a tentacle, gently touching DeepRunner, who turned one eye, ready to fight. But the larger kopri saw it was only OldFish, and kept working, sawing at the reeds while keeping one eye on OldFish.

"*How many lifetimes will it take,*" OldFish signed in neutral colors — gentle, kind and patient, "*to sink this floating island?*"

DeepRunner did not respond, beak plunging again and again into the reed cables, mantle turning gray with exhaustion.

OldFish's tentacle tip curled lightly around the nearest of DeepRunner's straining limbs — neither pushing nor pulling — just a gentle touch. A connection between two people.

Darkness flooded across DeepRunner, who retracted his beak into his mantle, tentacles releasing the Apum-ka and reaching toward OldFish. Entwining appendages, skin on skin, while bruised blue black sobbed over his mantle. Letting OldFish curl around him, embracing and comforting, as sorrow flashed and echoed over DeepRunner's skin.

Pink rimmed OldFish's eyes, a *Brooder's* gender emerging in the dark, as she held her grieving friend, whose flesh contracted, hard knots and ridges turning blue in despair. OldFish held tight, pink highlights ebbing lavender, until the blackness of DeepRunner's despair gave way — for the third time in his life — to a *Guardian's* gender, emerging in dark brown rings around his mantle.

"*We will find a way,*" OldFish signed. "*I have seen Kei. She lives, and all is not yet lost.*"

"*This is the end for me,*" DeepRunner flashed, "*I will sink to the bottom of the sea.*"

"*But not yet, dear friend,*" OldFish replied, "*You brought us here. We need you.*"

"*You saw her?*"

"*Yes, DeepRunner. I heard her voice. Strong and clear. She has not given up, and neither can we.*"

"*I want to take these beasts to the Deep with me,*" the old kopri brooder signed with a mix of anger and sadness.

"*Their island is too big,*" OldFish replied, blue calmness flowing over her skin. "*A single kopri would take a lifetime to tear it apart.*"

"*So we depend on a broken human to save us.*"

"*Only her body is broken, DeepRunner. Is our body what makes us people?*"

DeepRunner remained gray, no thoughts rising to his mantle. OldFish continued.

"*Four tentacles or eight. Our bodies are not who we are. She is Kei. She sings within our minds, and we sing in hers. That is what makes us people.*" OldFish signed, keeping her pink-tinged tentacles wrapped around DeepRunner, who relaxed into her embrace, his grief draining away.

"*What should I do?*" DeepRunner asked, his brown *Guardian* markings growing too dark to see. OldFish's mantle overflowed with rings of pink and yellow, her love entwining with hope. Her tentacle tips curled around DeepRunner, who returned the embrace. The couple clung to one another, there beneath the Apum-ka.

"*We wait, dearest friend,*" OldFish signed, "*And hope.*"

Why the Crying?

No senior officers came on deck the day after the *tayjaru* ceremony. But on the slaughter deck, work continued unabated, driven by the rise and fall of Koru-Kah cudgels — as junior officers vied to assert their dominance. During the hours of darkness, the immense trawling net had trailed behind the Apum-ka, gathering its victims. On this bright new morning, teams of enslaved na-manu drew it, length by length, from the sea. Slick silvery fish dropped to the slaughter deck, along with chunks of seaweed, white spindles of broken coral and a few kopri younglings, wordlessly flashing red alarm while gasping out their lives.

Beneath a pale blue sky, the slaughter resumed and blood flowed across the deck. Kei had now spent three weeks on the Apum-ka, floating northeast on the current. The days had grown cooler, but the sun still warmed Kei as she worked, weaving reed mats endlessly. Namaua sat nearby, fingers working the reeds, but neither woman spoke. Failure gripped Kei's tongue, while Namaua's shoulders sagged with exhaustion and too little sleep. Other women sat nearby, weaving, and Kei realized Namaua was the eldest of them. Not old, by the standards of Kei's village—but life on the Apum-ka was brutal and short. Those who failed to work were tossed overboard.

When the sun beat directly on Kei's head, both the guards and the na-manu paused their work for a break. The guards sat in a group, eating boiled tubers and steamed fish, served to them by servants with downcast eyes and slumping shoulders. The na-manu sat scattered on the deck, eating whatever raw bounty the sea provided.

Jacuti washed blood off his hands and carried a meal to his mother and Kei, who sat by their weaving on the far side of the debris shaft, near the center of the Apum-ka.

The food lay in a mound between them: strands of raw red algae scraped from the netting, and several fish carcasses stripped of their meaty fillets. The carcasses still held raw flesh in their tails, head and spine. Kei glanced at the debris shaft. Dozens of such carcasses had been tossed away, along with fish too small to bother with. But the guards had taken the kopri younglings—a delicacy to be preserved in crocks and sold at an enormous profit in the cities of the Koru-Kah, who wasted more than they harvested. They raped the sea and left ruin behind them, all for a few barrels of salted fish.

So much waste, Kei thought, as she picked up a glistening strand of red algae. At home in her village, people would have boiled the fish carcasses into a stew. She closed her eyes, mouth watering in memory of the rich aroma of fish stew, with wild scallions and coconut milk, served in bowls on the black sand beach of Tirahanko Bay. So long ago. Another lifetime.

The brine of raw algae wrinkled her nose.

"Its good," Jacuti said. As if to prove his point, he tipped back his head and dropped a long strand of algae into his mouth.

"It is called dulsu," Namaua added, "*Nutweed.* Better than kelp. Eat, Kei."

Kei glanced at the mound of red algae and picked up a strand.

"Dulsu," she sighed. But she mimicked Jacuti, leaning her head back and dropping the long damp strand into her mouth.

Salt exploded over her tongue as she chewed. The algae had the flavor of brine and waves. But as it fell apart in her mouth, it released a familiar flavor. Almost nutty, like roasted breadfruit, or cashews.

She plucked another long strand from the mound, surprised by how much she enjoyed the flavor.

The three ate in silence, with Jacuti and Namaua sucking eyeballs from the carcasses and nibbling delicate flesh from the top of the fish heads. Kei recoiled at the thought of eating a raw eyeball, the idea turning her stomach. Instead, she used a sharp reed to scrape the raw flesh from the spine of a butchered fish.

Each bite exploded in her mouth: firm and sweet, with a fresh ocean taste.

After they picked each carcass clean, Jacuti tossed them into the debris shaft, where they fell into the sea with a distant splash. Even that was a waste, Kei thought—the bones held so much flavor when boiled into broth.

They kept their voices low as they ate, speaking in whispers so no one could overhear. Nearby, other groups of dispirited na-manu sat in silence, picking at scraps, resting while mealtime offered a brief distraction from their ever-watchful guards.

"How will thee escape?" Namaua asked, slowly swallowing a piece of tender fish.

"We could just slip off the side of the Apum-ka," Kei said quietly.

"The guards would see us," Jacuti responded.

"Then we do it at night, when it's dark," Kei Replied.

"They lock us in the compound at night. I could climb the walls. But you. And my muhter?"

Kei's eyes dropped to her legs, and then to Namaua. The older woman was the same age as Kei's mother, but life on the Apum-ka was harsh. Even with the protection that being a Singer provided, Namaua had aged far beyond her years.

The older woman smiled at Kei. "No," Namaua said, "I could not make the climb either."

Namaua paused, then looked at Kei through eyes that saw a sad future. "How many kopri came with thee?"

"Two," Kei replied.

"Yes, I remember. Two."

Kei dropped her head, staring at the reed mats, but Namaua continued, "A full grown kopri can help a person swim. But not more than one." The older woman shook her head. "No, Kei, only the two of thee can escape. Even that may be too much for thy kopri to handle."

"Muhter!" Jacuti's breath exploded, his head shaking from side to side.

"My kayak," Kei said, her voice tight with frustration. "The koru-kah kept it. They've been trying to copy its design. Maybe the Kopri can bring it to us."

Namaua thought before replying, "even then, Kei, how much weight can thy friends tow? Thee must be out of sight before the sun rises. If the Koru-Kah can see thee from their lookout mast, they will send their fastest ship to catch thee. Bring thee back for punishment on the slaughter deck. Or execution, as an example to the others." Namaua's voice grew husky. "That was our mistake, Jacuti's father and I. We left too close to dawn and they spotted us." Her voice trailed off into sadness.

"No," Namaua said. Her voice low, firm. "Jacuti, thee cannot swim. A kopri will have to carry thee. And Kei's kayak will barely carry two—thee must be far beyond the horizon before daylight."

Jacuti's jaw opened. Closed. His cheeks flushed red. He glanced away from Namaua, at the water stretching behind the

Apum-ka. Jacuti had spent his life floating on the ocean's surface, but never once submerged into its bottomless embrace. He licked suddenly dry lips.

"Thee will go," Namaua told Jacuti. The tone in her voice allowed no argument. "If thee have a chance at freedom, thou must take it."

Jacuti shook his head, jaw clenching. His eyes flicked toward the Koru-Kah guards, at their cudgels and blades.

As if sensing her son's unspoken thoughts, Namaua sighed. She held Jacuti's eyes within her gaze, speaking softly. "I don't have long to live. But if thee escape, my life will be remembered."

"Thou knowest what will happen!" Jacuti said. "I can't let that happen to thee."

"I make my own choices, Jacuti. I always have. When I came here with DeepRunner—my choice. When I fell in love with a Koru-Kah officer—my choice. And when I stay here after thou leaveth—whatever happens—it will be my choice, not thine."

Silence fell between the mother and son. Jacuti squeezed his eyes shut, holding back tears. But his face drooped, shoulders slumping, as a trembling shook his chest and arms and hands. Then his eyes opened, but he could not face his mother. Instead, he reached forward and picked up the last of the carcasses, tossing it down the debris shaft.

"There is no way off the Apum-ka, anyway," Jacuti said. A splash echoed from the bottom of the debris shaft when the carcass hit the water.

Kei stared at the shaft. Her nose wrinkling.

Her eyes shifted toward the na-manu compound, where the Koru-Kah locked their enslaved workers at night.

Her lips turned downward, sourly.

"There are other waste shafts leading to the sea," she said, staring at the Na-manu quarters.

"The latrine shaft!" Jacuti said, nostrils flaring in memory of the stench of that pit, hidden by a reed screen in the farthest corner of the Na-manu quarters.

"It empties into the sea," Kei said, her brows narrowing.

"Thee want to jump down a latrine shaft?" Jacuti asked, horrified at the thought.

"Yes. It's near the edge of the Apum-ka. Near the open sea."

"I can't swim," Jacuti said, defeat gripping his voice.

"You live on a raft at sea," Kei said, keeping herself from shouting, "How can you not swim?"

Jacuti leaned back, lips pressed white together. But it was Namaua who spoke.

"This is not Nadako. Here, there are no gentle sand beaches. Waves would crush a swimmer against the side of the Apum-ka. And swimming serves no purpose for the Koru-Kah. Only rowing. Weaving. Butchering fish."

Kei nodded. Understanding, though frustration rimmed her eyes.

"I will steal a ship," Jacuti said, his eyes trailing out to sea.

"You can't row a Koru-Kah ship, just you and Kei," his mother said. "And the lookouts would see thee leaving. But

Kei's plan—thee won't have to swim—her kopri friends will help thee."

"Yes!" Kei agreed. "OldFish has untied and towed my kayak many times at home. All we have to do is speak to them ahead of time. They can be ready, waiting at the base of the shaft. The kopri are strong enough to carry both of us safely beneath the Apum-ka."

Jacuti swallowed a lump sticking in his throat as he thought about the gray darkness of the sea. His mother reached across the distance between them, placing a hand gently on her son's knee.

"Everything I sang to thee about the Kopri is true," she said. "If Kei sings to them, they will not let thee sink. Trust the Kopri, Jacuti, it is the only way."

Namaua turned to face Kei. "How will thee contact thy friends?"

Kei thought for many minutes, but no answer came to mind. It was Jacuti who responded.

"We will join a whaling boat. Kei is a strong rower. The two of us will volunteer together."

"Yes," Kei agreed. "OldFish will be looking for me. I'll sing to the Kopri and tell them our plan. Then we will slip into the sea at night, through the latrine hole. The kopri can untie my kayak and meet us. By morning, we will be out of sight of the Apum-Ka."

"And then what?" Jacuti asked, a frown darkening his face. He stared at his mother but found no relief in her tender gaze.

"I don't know," Kei said.

"Thee both shall return to Nadako!" Namaua's voice rang with steel. She turned to face Kei. "Take my son home. If thee don't escape, nothing will change. But if thee tell people what thou have learned, then maybe—"

"Muhter," Jacuti whispered, ashen-faced. "I can't abandon thee."

Namaua closed her eyes, calming herself. Preparing to sing. And when she did, the words of a lullaby soothed Jacuti, who scrunched his eyes together while his mother sang.

Little one, who sleeps on sand,
Beside the gentle sea.
Why the crying? Why the tears?
What brings the storm to thee?

Settle into slumber,
On a kayak filled with dreams.
O baby from the dry lands,
Thy life is out at sea.

Paddle, love, oh paddle,
On the oceans of my love.
Paddle, love, oh paddle,
On the oceans of my love.

When she finished singing, Namaua reached out once more, taking Jacuti's hand and squeezing until he opened his eyes. The two, mother and son, drank in one another's faces, memorizing every curve, every wrinkle, every errant strand of hair.

The decision had been made.

* * *

The next morning found the Koru-Kah senior officers on deck again, and the lookouts calling out excitedly from the crow's nest. A whale pod, cresting through ocean waves, shadowed the Apum-ka as it floated northeast with the current.

"They will take the hunting boat out," Jacuti said. He and Kei had come on deck early. Preparing for a chance like this. But Namaua had yet to leave the na-manu compound.

"I shouldst tell my muhter we're leaving," Jacuti said.

"There is no time," Kei replied. Jacuti frowned, then nodded his agreement.

They hurried over the reed mats. Dockside, Captain Ki-Kuna stood beside the small hunting boat. The harpooner had not yet arrived, nor had any other rowers. Ki-Kuna's face was paler than normal, with puffy bags beneath his eyes—a parting gift from the dead leafperson's *tayjaru* fungus. The Koru-Kah captain stared blankly at Jacuti and Kei as they crossed the dock to the side of the hunting boat. No expression other than weariness crossed Ki-Kuna's face as Kei approached.

"*Ai nuit atut* — " Jacuti said, bowing his body forward, eyes averted, explaining: "She rows well. And can sing while we harvest the whale."

Ki-Kuna's stone eyes drilled into Kei, who kept her face downcast, hiding her fear of being left behind. On the open sea, she could sing to her friends and read their sign. She could tell OldFish their plan for escape — to meet them tonight at the bottom of the latrine pit, to untie Kei's kayak and tow them to safety. She imagined the captain's cold eyes drilling into her skull. But then Ki-Kuna flicked his chin toward the hunting boat, ordering Kei aboard. She climbed in alongside Jacuti, then tucked her legs under the bench in front of her, preparing to row.

Shouts echoed over the top of the Apum-ka's hull, and soon other rowers jogged down the ramp, hastened by Koru-Kah cudgels. The harpooner boarded last, carrying his long, metal tipped spears.

"*Nauf!*" Ki-Kuna shouted, and the rowers dropped oars into water, while workers on the dock shoved the boat out to sea. With steady strokes, the hunting boat surged over the waves, towing Kei's kayak behind it. The Koru-Kah had recognized the value of her nimble craft — far more maneuverable than their heavy wooden rowboats — and had even begun replicating its design. But with none of their own completed, they had repaired Kei's own kayak and kept it close for their use.

Kei and Jacuti bent forward, pulling their oars in steady strokes, neither of them looking up at the top of the hull where Namaua stood, watching her son sail away.

Nor did they see a flash of gray jetting beneath the waves, as DeepRunner dove under the Apum-ka, heading to OldFish's listening post, beside the debris hole—to tell OldFish that Kei had come to sea!

The Deep

The hunting boat leapt across the water, unburdened by cargo. A thick-thewed Koru-Kah harpooner stood at the bow, seeking movement in the waves.

"What do we hunt?" Kei asked.

"They spotted a pod of pygmy whales." Jacuti grunted with effort, pulling the oar to his chest. "But they'll take whatever they find. Dolphin. Leafpeople. Kopri."

Captain Ki-Kuna shouted, silencing them. Kei left her horror unspoken: hunting kopri, as if her friends were mindless tuna! In Kei's time among the Koru-Kah, she had struggled to understand her captors. Her stomach twisted with a deep, gnawing ache whenever she thought of their incomprehensible cruelty. The image of Commander Té-Anka savoring a kopri youngling's flesh was never far from her mind. Despite her desire to make peace with the Koru-Kah, and save the kopri spawning grounds, she now thought of her Koru-Kah captors as beasts. As sharks. Not people at all.

Kei pulled the oar again and again, biceps burning with effort. Bright sun cut her eyes, which narrowed to slits as she scanned the ocean swells for any sign of her friends. Light glinted off wind-driven white caps, and blue water stretched away in every direction. The Apum-Ka receded to a tiny black dot on the horizon. Kei stared into the surrounding abyss, the weight of uncertainty pressing down on her. If she and Jacuti escaped, where would they go? She had no sense of where she was, or where they might find safety. The only certainty she had was the westward path of the sun, its steady journey the only guide she could trust.

But hope flared within her: once they escaped, she would have DeepRunner to guide them! The old kopri knew these waters, which were so near to the kopri spawning grounds.

Kei squeezed her eyes shut, blinking away salt spray and the blinding sun.

Food they could take from the sea. But water? How many days could she and Jacuti live without fresh water? Kei had never known privation. Her island home gave an abundance of the basics of life: water, fruit, fish from the sea. Strange, she had never noticed those simple blessings.

An image of her father's hut, at the edge of his small cove, floated through her mind. Near the hut, a small sweet-water stream fed into the cove. She had drunk from that stream every day without thinking—paying no attention to the wealth that blessed her.

Kei licked dry, flaking lips. Parched and shriveled. The Koru-Kah gave their enslaved workers only the minimum water needed to survive. And its taste! Stored in resin-soaked barrels, then passed around in leather drinking bladders. Her tongue flicked over her upper lip, but to no effect. Her mouth was dry as sunbaked sand, tongue puffy and rasping.

She pressed her mouth into a white puckering line, darting her eyes across the endless waves. Her arms moved in a circular rhythm, pulling the oar back through the water until her hands touched her chest. Then pushing down to lift the oar from the water, arms thrusting forward in a circular sweep which ended with the oars dropping into the waves behind her. And then the burn of biceps, shoulders, back and stomach as her whole body pulled the oar, stiff legs braced under the bench in front of her, rowing in unison along with the other oar-slaves on the boat.

Drop. Pull. Lift. Repeat.

Drop. Pull. Lift. Repeat.

But then suddenly the cycle was interrupted. The oar quivered as it struck the waves.

Vibrating.

Dragging slowly through the water.

A shadow lurked beneath the waves—hugging the smooth wood planks of the boat hull. One tentacle gripped the moving end of Kei's oar, then released its hold as the kopri mantle contracted, and her dearest friend, OldFish, kept hidden from all eyes but hers. Kei kept her face turned forward, watching the water from the corner of her eye, giving her captors no sign that a kopri kept pace with their lumbering boat.

OldFish thrust one ear-knob above the water's surface, its body hidden against the submerged hull of the ship. Kei smiled and began to sing in the words of the Nadako.

She entertained the Koru-Kah with a song in a language her captors couldn't understand, all the while weaving her plan for escape into the melody she shared with OldFish.

* * *

Swimming deep beneath Kei and OldFish, DeepRunner contracted his mantle, sending a jet of water behind him as he matched the lumbering speed of the Koru-Kah hunting boat. Violet flashes of derision arced along his tentacles: these beasts! These humans of the floating islands! They clung to the ocean surface like blooms of kelp, helpless, going wherever the current took them. Or floundering in their giant kayaks, like the one lurching through the waves above him.

DeepRunner angled an eye upward at the darkened bottom of the boat's hull, which blotted out the sun, its movement an inky stain creeping across the glowing surface of the world. For a moment, the shadow passing over pulled him back in time, reminding him of the long-ago shadow that had fallen over his nest and his first mate, SwimsAbove. Sadness rippled blue across his mantle. Try as he might to suppress it, a wave of grief for his lost love swept over him, pulling him into a brief despair. Then, just as swiftly, it was gone, leaving him drained and alone.

But then, a ripple in the water broke through the stillness. DeepRunner swiveled his other eye, focusing on the movement. There. OldFish. Jetting downward toward him. The smaller kopri's mantle contracted, glowing with indigo excitement. DeepRunner tracked her descent with one eye, while the other remained fixed on the Koru-Kah hull, which now, strangely, reminded him of a clamshell.

DeepRunner turned from OldFish, both eyes stabbing upward at the boat's hull. Yes. It was no different from a clamshell, except that its wooden planks were softer, more vulnerable than the stony casing of a clam.

DeepRunner snapped his beak shut to a razor point, a pulse of red flashing over his mantle. He had drilled through countless shells, prying open the defenses of many tender clams to claim them from the safety of their homes.

Then OldFish floated beside him, her signs glowing in the dim light, there beneath the Koru-Kah boat.

"Kei sang to me. She has a plan!" OldFish signed. *"She will leave tonight. We are to wait by the small waste shaft, furthest from the boat docks. She will drop down to us."*

DeepRunner rippled green around his eyes, acknowledging that he understood.

"But she asks something from you," OldFish signed.

"What?"

"She brings another human with her. She asks that you carry him tonight."

"One of the beasts?"

"No. A friend. The child of Namaua, who you brought here long ago."

DeepRunner dropped to silent gray. Namaua. Memory dripped blue over his skin. So many cycles of the current. A weariness settled into his tentacles. But then green rippled around his eyes, agreeing. Understanding.

"You will carry him out from under the floating island," OldFish said, *"He cannot swim."*

"It will weigh me down. Like a dead log."

"Not for long. You must just take him to the kayak."

Weariness settled into DeepRunner—his end time was so near. Orange knobs rose around his eyes.

"Namaua?" he asked.

"I don't know."

More turquoise questions began flashing along DeepRunner's tentacles, but then the rhythm of the Koru-Kah oars changed. The black stain on the surface of the world shifted direction.

DeepRunner's eyes turned, following the Koru-Kah ship's new heading.

OldFish turned silent gray, looking up as well. The Koru-Kah oars dropped and pulled, driving their boat toward an object floating in the sea.

Both kopri saw the Koru-Kah's new target: the floating body of a leafperson—from which a kopri youngling dangled, flashing rainbow specks of laughter while its mantle pushed above the waves, nibbling blue *tayjaru* fungus.

DeepRunner's skin suddenly burned with the bold red of human blood. Anger seethed, grief and rage driving new strength into ancient tentacles grown weak with too many cycles of the current. Too many years seeking to save his people. The Deep beckoned, but the sight above him pushed darkness away and filled him once more with power.

In unison, DeepRunner and OldFish contracted their mantles, jetting upward toward the leafperson body. Racing to beat the Koru-Kah to the unsuspecting child reveling in its newfound, *tayjaru*-fueled intelligence.

* * *

The minutes stretched on as Kei rowed, her arms burning from the effort, but the excitement of knowing she had told OldFish her plan kept her going. Just as that feeling began to calm her, the harpooner's voice shouted, full of excitement, as he pointed at the water and readied his wicked spear. The captain's voice rose, issuing clipped orders that sent the ship churning toward a small dark blotch floating on the waves. As the hunting boat approached, Ki-Kuna shouted more orders. The Harpooner set down his spear and moved toward the rear of the boat—where Kei's kayak trailed. A bundled net with a spooled line hung over the harpooner's shoulder.

"Leafperson!" Jacuti whispered. Kei looked across the water and saw the length of the leafperson bobbing on the waves, wings floating on either side.

"*Uscht!*" Ki-Kuna barked, "*Stop!*" Kei shipped her oar. The boat slowed to a halt, a stone's throw from the leafperson.

Behind her, the kayak's tether slithered into the sea. The Harpooner set paddle to water and sent Kei's kayak gliding across the ocean.

Kei's stomach clenched when she looked at the leafperson, and at the fringes of blue *tayjaru* fungus growing along its fibrous body. But the fungus was not the reason her breath caught. Attached to the leafperson, nibbling blue fungus and glowing a contented yellow, a kopri youngling clung— oblivious to the harpooner darting toward it.

The harpooner grinned as he swung the net above his head and cast it, trapping the child within its coils.

The yellow happiness on the youngling's mantle flashed to black, fear consuming its infant mind.

A grin split the harpooner's face as the net dropped across the leafperson body and he began pulling in the line—drawing leafperson, *tayjaru* and tender kopri morsel toward him.

Kei leaned forward, feet trapped beneath the bench in front of her. Stone silence filled Jacuti's face. There was nothing they could do but watch.

The sun pummeled Kei's face. Her shoulders ached. The hunting ship bobbed on the waves.

And then time came to a stop, sunlight dazzling Kei's eyes as the world seemed to freeze.

The harpooner's hand was outstretched, reaching for the youngling, drops of water falling from his hands. The youngling clung motionless. Black as night. Joy turned to terror.

And when a wave slapped the hull, starting time again — the koru-kah was gone — pulled to the Deep by a blood red tentacle constricting around the harpooner's arm, dragging him into the sea.

The NetSinger

aptain Ki-Kuna stared at the rippling water, his gaze fixed on the fungus-covered leafperson body, still tangled in the net.

Then the surface erupted. The harpooner's face broke through, gasping desperately for air — only to be seized again, suckered tentacles wrapping tight and yanking him back into the depths.

Ki-Kuna leaned forward, scanning the water, his eyes sharp, searching.

Minutes passed. Then, slowly, the harpooner's body surfaced, face down, bobbing lifeless on the waves.

The captain's eyes turned to slits as he barked orders. A Koru-Kah warrior picked up a second spear, casting it into the body of the leafperson where the youngling still clung, tangled in the net.

From her rowing bench, Kei saw motion beneath the waves. Then two tentacles reached up, struggling to release the child. OldFish!

But the Koru-Kah hauled in their line, dragging the leafperson and youngling toward the ship.

Tears formed in Kei's eyes as OldFish struggled with the knots, trying to free the terrified child.

"Watch out!" She sang without thinking. A Koru-Kah sailor — standing at the railing — threw a third spear toward OldFish.

Then the water exploded as a red mass of enraged kopri burst over the ship's railing. DeepRunner's tentacles lashed around the spear thrower's head, his massive mantle crashing onto the deck. His trailing limbs spilled over the railing, razor-edged suckers biting into the wooden planks.

The spearman screamed. A long wail suddenly ending with a snap, as his head doubled backward in the grip of angry red tentacles. Captain Ki-Kuna leapt forward, long knife glinting in harsh sunlight as the captain slashed DeepRunner. A tentacle, still wrapped around the spearman's head, sliced off cleanly. But the severed end coiled around the limp sailor's neck, its tiny mind gripping tight, even as it died. DeepRunner flushed in agony, his remaining limbs thrashing as he heaved himself over the railing and plunged back into the sea.

The leafperson body floated free on the waves, still wrapped in netting, but no longer tethered to the ship. Kei's kayak floated away as well. Ki-Kuna shouted orders and the drum beat resumed. Oars dropped into waves as the ship turned to pursue OldFish, who was towing the trapped youngling and leafperson away.

Kei's knuckles whitened as she gripped her oar, heart pounding. Hands stilled. Refusing to row. Then a Koru-Kah club smashed into her shoulder. Shards of fire lanced through her body, jolting her arms. In shock, Kei dropped her oar into the water, pulling backward with tears stinging her cheeks. Nearby, Jacuti's face darkened, anger pulsing through fists and arms. His eyes narrowed, staring at the drawn blades of his enslavers, reflecting diamond light along their razor edges. Against the wicked knives and heavy clubs of the Koru-Kah, he was helpless to act—without meeting his father's fate.

Ki-Kuna held his long knife out, glaring at his enslaved rowers and shouting orders as he turned his ship to pursue the fleeing kopri.

The boat began moving forward again. Ki-Kuna ordered the dead spearman tossed overboard. The body floated away, with DeepRunner's severed tentacle still constricted around the corpse's neck.

But DeepRunner had seven more tentacles, and one shot out of the sea—wrapping around an oar and wrenching it from the shocked grip of the enslaved na-manu.

Ki-Kuna yelled, and the guards rained blows onto the rowers, forcing their oars to keep moving. Twice more, throbbing red tentacles exploded from the sea, yanking oars from the hands of the unresisting na-manu. Ki-Kuna bared his teeth, waving his knife in frustration, then shouted an order: *"Tomay — Ship oars!"*

The rowers willingly pulled in their oars, letting the ship float to a stop.

More shouts. More orders, and the boat's single sail unfurled and raised to catch the wind.

Ki-Kuna faced the open sea, his eyes locked on the leafperson body being towed further out of reach, with the squirming youngling still struggling to free itself from the net.

Wind filled the sail, and Ki-Kuna's ship surged forward, closing the gap to his receding prey.

Then a vibration shuddered through the hull, ripples coursing through the stinking bilge water pooled beneath the rowers' feet.

A harder jolt followed, something striking the bottom of the boat — something solid, sharp, and full of rage.

Behind Kei and Jacuti, a Koru-Kah steersman gripped the tiller, guiding the boat forward under the full power of a straining sail. The steersman grunted with effort, his hands tight on the tiller as he kept the course straight, sailing directly toward OldFish and the struggling youngling.

A sudden gust of wind slammed into the sail, knocking the ship off course. The steersman cursed under his breath, fighting to turn into the wind and regain control.

"Ka hemah! Heilah!" Ki-Kuna shouted, enraged. *"Right bank, Turn!"*

But the sail billowed out with the wind, refusing to be tamed, and the ship angled further from its course.

Ki-Kuna turned, preparing to assist his steersman, but before he could take another step toward the tiller, the deck trembled. Sea water surged into the bilge, rushing up from beneath and flooding into the ship.

Ki-Kuna whipped his head around. His eyes widened as a kopri beak burst through the deck, striking again and again, ripping a gash into the hull that spewed seawater.

Uttering a curse, Ki-Kuna threw himself toward the hole, desperate, uncaring. His long knife flashed, plunging through the opening and striking kopri flesh.

The vibration stopped and blue-tinged water welled up through the wide hole, followed by a torrent of seawater that threatened to sink the ship. Guards and na-manu grabbed buckets, bailing scoop after scoop of water. But it was a losing battle. The hole ripped into the hull by DeepRunner's sharp beak was too large to plug. The ocean flooded into the Koru-Kah ship, unstoppable.

The ship lurched, the tiller flailing wildly. Kei turned, adrenaline shivering across her skin when she saw silent gray tentacles pulling the steersman overboard. Then OldFish surged from the sea, the tiny kopri youngling gripping her mantle with desperate strength. OldFish wrapped tentacles around the tiller, turning the ship into a gusting wind as water fountained madly through the hull.

"Jump Kei!" OldFish signed, before slipping back below the waves.

The mast began leaning toward the ocean, the sail flapping wildly in the wind. Screams filled Kei's ears as the na-manu rowers panicked, some leaping into the sea and clutching their floating oars—safe for now. Others clung to the railing, frozen in fear. Kei noticed, like a distant memory, that several Koru-Kah guards had toppled over the railing and were being swept under the waves—like Jacuti, the Koru-Kah had never learned to swim.

But then, there was OldFish, floating on the water, waiting.

"Jacuti, over here!" Kei shouted, pulling herself off the rowing bench and dragging her legs over the ship's railing. Cold water slammed into her, jolting the breath from her lungs as she plunged into the roiling sea. With practiced strokes, her hands reached upward, pulling her toward the surface, gasping for air as she struggled toward her kayak.

Jacuti clung to the side of the capsizing ship, eyes widening as he stared into the bottomless water threatening to swallow him whole.

Nearby, Captain Ki-Kuna stood at the tilting railing, defiantly pointing his long knife toward Jacuti, shouting orders as he struggled to save his doomed ship. His voice rose in harsh commands, but then he turned sharply as a boiling sound erupted behind him.

DeepRunner!

One severed tentacle retracted uselessly into the old kopri's mantle, where a wound poured blue blood while his ancient scar throbbed brilliant red. With the last of his strength, DeepRunner jetted out of the water, reaching for the captain. Ki-Kuna leapt from the overturning deck, knife flashing, striking at the demon kopri that sought to kill him.

DeepRunner and Ki-Kuna embraced, knife point driving deep, tentacles constricting. The deck heaved beneath them, tilting as wooden planks groaned in protest.

Jacuti's wild eyes stared at DeepRunner and the Captain, his hands clutching the railing. Then Kei's voice echoed up from the treacherous water:

"Jacuti! Over here! Jump!" Kei shouted.

Jacuti turned and spotted her in the dark water, her arms churning wildly to keep her head above the waves. Then OldFish surged from the water, coiling a tentacle around Kei's waist and lifting her free of the swirling sea and pushing her toward her kayak. The ship groaned again, its hull creaking as the deck slipped toward the waves, dragging Jacuti closer to the deep.

Screaming buffeted his ears, his stomach heaving with the rolling waves. The ship's deck turned into a wall behind him, rising above the water. Jacuti lost his footing, plunging into the sea, along with several other rowers — who grabbed oars and wood debris. As cold water filled Jacuti's nose and mouth, the other rowers clutched floating wreckage, finding temporary safety, but Jacuti flailed, no oars or crates or barrels nearby. The brine sucked him under, and in moments his head throbbed, lungs screaming for air. Then Jacuti felt something slither around his waist, pushing him out of the water. Salt burned his nose and lips as he gasped violently, life exploding into his lungs.

The mast crashed into the sea. The ship overturned, sending out cresting waves.

Then, all was silent.

* * *

Salt stung Jacuti's eyes, but he kept them open as Kei's kayak approached. Screams battered his ears, from guards clinging to the overturned ship. But OldFish held him safe, keeping his weight from dragging him down to a watery death.

The kayak slid alongside him, and he reached up, grasping Kei's hand as she struggled to pull him aboard. He floundered, terror of the sucking depths nearly overcoming him. Desperate, he flung his other arm across the bow, tilting the kayak dangerously. Then the Kopri's tentacle tightened around his waist, heaving him upward. OldFish surged from the water, tossing Jacuti onto the kayak before vanishing beneath the waves.

"You are safe," Kei said. Jacuti heard her soft voice, which cut through terror and calmed the panic swirling through his mind. Still gasping, he lay helpless on the front of the kayak, while Kei sat astride its stern, paddling.

He glanced back at the hunting ship, at the struggling forms clinging to its overturned hull, and the enslaved na-manu, held above the waves by oars and other wooden debris. He quickly counted his na-manu companions—most of whom had not grown up on an Apum-ka like him, and knew how to swim.

One thick-armed woman swam to a sinking na-manu and pushed an oar into his flailing hands. Together, the woman and the man she saved floated beside the overturned ship, waiting for rescue. Jacuti realized that most, or maybe all, of the na-manu had survived the wreck, as had most of the Koru-Kah. As Jacuti watched, the hunting boat's first mate crawled onto the overturned hull and stood up, shouting orders.

Jacuti turned his head and saw a kopri tentacle tip gripping the reeds of the kayak's upcurved bow, which shot over the waves faster than Kei could paddle. The kopri jetted steadily, mantle contracting, towing Kei and Jacuti to safety.

As OldFish towed the kayak, the kopri youngling clung to her mantle, terror subsiding to green comfort, as OldFish stroked its small mantle with a caressing tentacle tip, flashing a green *sign* of greeting. The youngling hesitantly copied the sign, awareness blossoming in the child's newly formed mind.

Eventually, Jacuti sat upright and took a turn with the paddle. Few words passed between Kei and Jacuti as they focused on escape. Far in the distance, a tiny black dot—the Apum-ka—faded into the horizon.

"We must get out of sight," Jacuti said, "before their rescue ships reach the wreck."

"You think more boats will come?" Kei asked between breaths as she paddled.

"Yah. The Koru-Kah will come. To recover their *na-manu*. Their *property*."

"I think all of the other rowers survived," Kei replied.

Then silence enveloped them as Kei and Jacuti paddled toward their freedom. Once out of sight, the Koru-Kah would never find them; in the vastness of the open ocean, they could vanish. And so they paddled, while OldFish towed the kayak.

After half the day passed, they pulled their paddle from the water, while OldFish floated beside them, exhausted. Only the youngling sparkled, delighted by the *newness* of the world.

OldFish, Kei, Jacuti and the baby kopri were dots in an endless expanse of blue.

No ships shadowed the horizon.

No islands or land rose into the sky.

The Apum-ka was nowhere in sight.

Just Jacuti and Kei, floating on endless blue. And OldFish, with the small youngling clinging to her mantle. The youngling glowed yellow, eyestalks swiveling to follow the patterns flashing on OldFish's skin as the adult kopri spoke to Kei — who translated for Jacuti as they talked.

"Where is DeepRunner?" Kei asked, singing high and clear so OldFish could hear.

"*He has gone to the Deep,*" OldFish replied. Kei interpreted the kopri signs for Jacuti, which dripped like blue tears down OldFish's tentacles.

"DeepRunner? The giant kopri?" Jacuti asked. His voice shook. He had lived his entire life on a floating island and the endless expanse of deadly water around him sucked away his bravery. Sharp breaths threatened his voice, but he continued, "I saw him. When the ship turned over. He had his tentacles wrapped around the Captain. They both went under while the Captain drove his knife into the kopri. I didn't see them come back up."

"DeepRunner is gone," OldFish confirmed, wrapping a tentacle gently around Kei's hand. *"The Prophet's time has ended."*

Together, OldFish and Kei mourned the passing of their friend. After a time though, Kei smiled, seeing yellow crinkles around the youngling's eyes, where it clung to OldFish.

"Hello little youngling," Kei sang, as slow and clearly as she could. OldFish flashed a greeting sign, which the youngling mimicked.

"It doesn't really understand," OldFish signed, pink circles forming around her eyes. *"Its mind is too new. But its learning."*

Kei said nothing, but she nodded, understanding. She had watched mothers teaching speech to toddlers many times. OldFish's interaction with the youngling was no different. So many things had become clear to her, only now, when she floated helpless in the vastness of the world.

"Which way do we go?" Jacuti asked, overwhelmed by the surrounding emptiness. "Where is the Nadako Sea?"

"I'm not going home, to Nadako," Kei replied.

Jacuti remained silent. Bobbing up and down on ceaselessly rolling waves, until Kei spoke again.

"I came here to save the Kopri. I promised DeepRunner I would sing for them."

"You did that," Jacuti replied. "But the Koru-Kah refused to listen."

"We tried," OldFish agreed, *"But now it is time to go home. We will find another way."*

"We already have," Kei said, laughter spilling from her lips and pouring out over the waves. OldFish rippled orange and turquoise, questioning. Jacuti merely stared.

Kei shook with laughter. She bent forward, eyes closing as her chest shook. The laughter deepened, turning to a sob. And then silence. Finally, she looked up again, all mirth gone. And all grief once more safely pressed into darkness, deep within herself.

"DeepRunner told me, back in Tirahanko Bay. But I didn't understand then. He didn't either. Don't you remember, OldFish? DeepRunner said *the minds of our younglings light with thought no more."*

"Yes," OldFish agreed. *"The Koru-Kah disturb our spawning grounds, and our younglings starve, remaining mindless, unable to speak."*

"But why, OldFish? What makes that happen? Why do they stay mindless?"

OldFish turned gray, eyes blinking.

"That youngling clinging to you. You said it yourself — its mind is new. But its body must have been born months ago, to be that large. So why does its mind spark with color only now? What happened to set its intelligence blazing?"

OldFish reached a tentacle toward the youngling, gently stroking its mantle. The youngling shivered pink with happiness, flashing its newly learned greeting-sign repeatedly.

"The Koru-Kah told me," Kei said, "That's the funny thing. They try to eat the world. They refused to hear me. But the Koru-Kah themselves told me the truth."

Kei turned to Jacuti, asking, "The fungus harvested from the decaying bodies of leafpeople. What do the Koru-Kah call it?"

"*Tayjaru*," Jacuti replied without thinking, "The giver of mind."

"The Giver of Mind!" Kei's notes soared out over the ocean. "Don't you see, OldFish? That youngling on your mantle was eating *tayjaru*! And now its mind sparks with life. It's not just how much food your younglings have. It's the fungus. We just saw it happen. That youngling clinging to you just ate *tayjaru*, and now its mind sparkles with new intelligence. But since the Koru-Kah have come, they harvest the leafpeople and all the blue fungus. You don't need to convince the Koru-Kah of anything. You need to speak to the Leafpeople. What you need is *tayjaru* — and *the gift of mind* it sparks."

Kei let her voice fall silent, and for a time the kayak bobbed on the undulating sea. Until Kei sang again, conviction and certainty giving power to her notes.

"We are not going home to Nadako. Namaua told me the leafpeople dwell in the south, on the slopes of Mount Urkpry. That's where we have to go. To seek the aid of the Leafpeople and find the source of *Tayjaru*. Then we can light the minds of all the younglings once more!"

Kei smiled, stretching her stiffened legs across the kayak's reeds. She placed one hand on OldFish's tentacle, and reached the other to Jacuti, feeling the warmth of his palm on hers.

Then she took up her paddle.

And the NetSinger's own journey began.

< the end >

Kei's story concludes in
Tide Song: Children of Tayjaru
Available now on Amazon

If you enjoyed Kei's adventure,
please leave a review.

Reviews are the best way to help other
readers find new worlds to enjoy.

Appendix One: Characters

Characters	Role
Ahmisha *ah-MEE-sha*	Kei's mother. Leader of the Singers and Choir, responsible for communicating with the Kopri during official meetings and other events.
DeepRunner *DEEP-run-ner*	Ancient kopri, regarded as a prophet by the other kopri
Jacuti *cha-COO-tee*	Son of Namaua whose name means: "Eyes that hear the world"
Kei *KEY*	Common Nadako girl's name, derived from fire, "kea", and ice, "in." The name translates as "the balance between fire and ice, all things in harmony"
Ki-Kuna *ki-KU-nah*	Captain of a Koru-Kah supply ship, son of Commander Té-Anka
Namaua: *NA-mauw-ah*	Jacuti's mother, from Meransi, the many islands
OldFish *OLD-fish*	Kei's closest friend. OldFish's kopri sign-name is an untranslatable pattern involving yellow and green ripples, with orange pulses around their eyes.
Té-Anka *tay-AHN-ka*	Commander of the Apum-Ka. Ki-Kuna's father.

Appendix Two: Kopri Sign Translations

Sign/Emotion	pattern/description
Agreement *Green*	Quick rippling green flashes spreading across the mantle
Amusement *All colors*	Steady glowing multi-colors
Anger *Red, dark*	Dark red, smooth and steady
Annoyance *Black and gray*	Black and gray edging on other signs, indicating annoyance as they speak.
Applause *Orange*	Flashing rhythmic orange spirals around the eyes
Comfort/Sympathy *Brown and blue*	Field of brown skin, with blue dots and streaks
Command *Purple, pulsing*	Steady deep purple, or a deep purple with pulses to black
Decisiveness *Purple, knobs*	Ring of purple knobs surrounding the eyes
Denial, innocence *Light Gray, nearly white*	Entire mantle turns white
Despair *Gray-Black*	Smooth gray-black on every part of body
Excitement *Violet*	Entire mantle glows light violet, flashing on and off with the degree of excitement
Exhaustion *Dark gray/black*	A deep gray covering the entire body, sometimes with streaks of black in random patterns

Fear *Jet black*	The entire body turns a deep jet black
Greeting *All colors*	Mantle with crenulated knobs across all its surface, with rainbow colors flashing
Laughter *All colors*	All colors randomly flashing on and off in random smooth patterns across the entire mantle
Love *Pink*	Highlights edging other signs, or as a gentle glowing across the body
Names *Varies*	Patterns of light and ridges scrunched into mantles, unique to each kopri
Pain *Crimson Red*	Bright red splotches, knobs and ridges, flashing randomly, or rising as crenulations across a portion of the body, glowing very bright crimson red
Pride *Pink and Yellow*	Alternating pink and yellow rings, surrounding other signs or rippling down the mantle
Questioning *Orange and Turquoise*	Alternating bumps of orange and turquoise forming a ring around the eyes
Readiness/serenity *Turquoise*	Steady and smooth turquoise glow across the mantle
Resignation *Black and blue*	Streaks of black and blue running down mantle and tentacles
Sadness *Blue*	Dark blue crinkling skin
Silence *Gray, light*	Smooth light gray skin, featureless in every way
Smile *Yellow*	Spiraling yellow around the eyes

Appendix Three: Koru-Kah Translations

Koru-Kah Word	Translation
Ah-en: *ah-EN*	You
Anah: *AW-nah*	Please
Apum-ka: *AH-pume-KA*	Floating Island Home
Ar-Kora: *ar-KOR- rah*	A Koru-Kah colony
Atūt: *ah-toot*	Great, powerful, important
Atūt-Mā: *ah-toot mah*	"Great One," or "slave master"
Aulöla *(AW-loo-lah)*	Full, complete
Ayen: *ia-en*	She
Graateh: *gray-tay*	Speed
Heilah: *hile-A*	Turn
Hekeh: *hay-keh*	Plea
Hemah: *heh-mah*	Bank
Himene: *hei-meyn-ee*	Tonight
Kahrre: *KAH-ahr-reh*	Cannot
Keetuh: *kee-tuh*	Overboard
Lohmeh: *low-meh*	Drop
Mā: *mah*	One who is powerful
Māhk: *mock*	Eat/consume
Māhn: *mahn*	Now/present
Maih: *mai*	From

Mascht: *ma-sh-t*	Learn, discover
Na-manu: *nah-mah-noo*	Less than a man, fit only for labor
Ome: *oh-meh*	Enlighten me
Rue: *roo-ee*	Take
Schprekinneh: *schpreh-ken-neh*	Song
Schrehtani: *Schreh-tahn-ee*	Hear/listen
Schrenku: *SCHREN-koo*	Sing
T': *tee*	Implies the opposite
Tacheh: *tah-chey*	Throw
Tahn: *tahn*	You
Tayjaru: *tay-jar-rue*	Giver of Mind
Tehoss: *TAY-hohs*	Oars
To: *toh*	Our
Tohchrah: *TOHK-rah*	Anchor
Tomay: *toh-may*	Raise
Torrah: *tor-RAH*	Dies/death
Tureba: *too-reh-bah*	Bring
Tutacheh: *too-tah-kee*	Beg/plead
Uscht: *ue-SCH-t*	Stop
Varhneh: *varn-eh*	Woman
Watatachi: *wah-tah-tah-chee*	Of value, worth keeping
Yamahuni: *yama-who-ni*	A derogatory Koru-Kah curse

Appendix Four: Nadako Translations

Nadako Word	Meaning
Agu: *AH-goo*	Wet
Aguerde: *AH-gwer-day*	A vast mangrove saltwater swamp separating Nadako from Menehko
Ansi: *AHN-see*	Island
Anziko: *AHN-zee-koh*	An island in the Eastern Sea
Cuti: *KOO-tee*	Hear
Eba: *EH-bah*	Servant
Erde: *ER-day*	Land/dirt
Erdwala: *ERD-wah-lah*	Wildlands
Iba: *EE-bah*	North
In: *EEN*	Ice
Inko: *EEN-koh*	Ocean of Ice
Ja: *JAH*	Eye
Ji: *JEE*	West
Jikea: *JEE-kayah*	Name of a volcano, translates as "Western Fire"
Kea: *KAY-ah*	Fire

Keako: *KAY-ah-koh*	"Ocean Fire," a volcano on the eastern marshland shores
Kiz: *KIZ*	Woman
Ko: *KOH*	Ocean
Ko-Erda: *ko-AIR-dah*	Land and the sea, the world.
Koeba: *KOH-eh-bah*	Servants of the ocean
Kop: *KOHP*	Mouth
Koperda: *koh-PER-dah*	Wild kopri, incapable of communication
Kopri: *KOH-pree*	Valued partners of the Nadako people, intelligent octopus
Kopzkiko: *KOPS-kee-koh*	Mouth of the eastern sea
Koru-Kah: *core-rue-KAH*	Slavers of the East
Meneh: *MEH-neh*	Big, large
Menehko: *MEH-neh-koh*	Great Ocean
Mer: *MEHR*	Many
Meransi: *MEHR-ahn-see*	Land of Many Islands

Mt. Urkpry: *mount URK-pree*	Volcanic mountain dominating the southern lands. Translates as "Mountain of the Leafpeople"
Na: *NAH*	Small, little, nothing
Nadako: *NAH-dah-koh*	The little ocean
Na-manu: *NAH-mah-noo*	Less than a man, fit only for labor
Preba *PRE-bah*	Name used by Kei's people for themselves
Pri: *PREE*	Possessing personhood
Pry: *PRY*	People
Rapeo: *RAH-peh-oh*	South
Ru: *ROO*	Kingdom, village, or Our Home
Ruedeba *RU-dee-bah*	The place a Singer stands to converse with the Kopri
Singer: *SING-er*	Head of the Singer's Enclave-elected tribal leader
Tirahanko: *teer-ah-HAN-koh*	Harbor, shelter from the sea
Ur: *OOR*	Leaf
Urkpry: *URK-pree*	Leaf People
Zi: *ZEE*	East

Book Club Questions

1. What did you appreciate most about the world-building created by the book, and how did that affect your experience of the story?

2. What did you think of the way the Kopri communicated? How did their unique methods of interaction (e.g., color changes, body language) shape the story?

3. Why do the Koru-Kah feel they have the right to take everything in the ocean?

4. How did you feel about SwimsAbove in the Koru-Kah net? How did you feel about the regular fish caught in Kei and the Kopri's net in the first hunt?

5. Like the colorful kopri, apes can use sign language and also, whales communicate with one another. Should apes, whales, and kopri have the same rights as humans?

6. Why is OldFish so loyal to Kei?

7. Are Kei's people servants of the Kopri? Why or why not?

8. DeepRunner said,"*They are just humans. Just useful prey. If they won't hunt for me, then I will take them with me to the deep.*" What changed DeepRunner's mind about humans?

9. If you lived among these octopuses, what aspects of their culture would be the hardest or easiest to adapt to?

10. What did you think of the way the author handled relationships — friendships, family, or romance?

11. Which characters in the novel are people? Why?

12. How does Kei's accident on the reef at the age of 9 affect her life?

13. Did you relate to the protagonist's struggles or choices? Why or why not?

14. How do you think Jacuti feels about his parentage?

15. What thoughts do you have about DeepRunner's final acts?

16. The book ends with this: "Then she took up her paddle. And the Netsinger's own journey began." What does Kei possess at the end of the book that she didn't have in the beginning?

17. If you could change one event in the story, what would it be and why?

About the Author

K. E. Hummel is a disability rights advocate, English professor and grandfather, who believes all people matter. After 30 years managing programs helping people with disabilities lead empowered lives, Hummel is currently "seasonally retired," and working in the public school system with students with autism & emotional support needs. Living with his wife and editor, Joanie Lorraine, Hummel spends his time writing, educating, and telling the grandkids stories about the good old days, back when he was a young pirate sailing the seas and fighting dragons. His stories challenge readers to go beyond their limitations and control their own destinies. All you need is faith in yourself, and the courage to dream.